ACT OF *Love*

PAN ZADOR

CRIMSON ROMANCE
F+W Media, Inc.

Published by
Crimson Romance
an imprint of F+W Media, Inc.
10151 Carver Road, Suite 200
Blue Ash, Ohio 45242

www.crimsonromance.com

Copyright © 2012 by Pan Zador

ISBN 10: 1-4405-6137-0
ISBN 13: 978-1-4405-6137-5
eISBN 10: 1-4405-6138-9
eISBN 13: 978-1-4405-6138-2

This is a work of fiction. Names, characters, corporations, institutions, organizations, events, or locales in this novel are either the product of the author's imagination or, if real, used fictitiously. The resemblance of any character to actual persons (living or dead) is entirely coincidental.

For Nico
who cherishes me with laughter and music, onstage and off.

CHAPTER ONE

"You're too small for the part," said Tor Douglas. "Ridiculously small, if you don't mind my saying so."

Marigold felt her face burning as he delivered these lines in an emphatic, deep voice. His enormous frame sprawled in a large swivel chair as he sized her up with an amused expression.

Glancing around the walls of his office, which was covered in posters from previous productions of the Tower Theatre Company, she couldn't help seeing the names of well-known actors—women and men she had admired as a stage-struck child. But now, she was a graduate, an actor, a professional like them—how dare he dismiss her, unheard!

Taking a deep breath before she spoke, as she had been taught, she acted confident—though she felt anything but. Never before had her training been so useful. Her first real audition, and she was being shown the door by this patronizing, horrible man!

"Let me at least show you what I can do," she said with her chin in the air.

He raised a lazy, challenging eyebrow.

"I've two pieces prepared...and a song..." Her voice began to falter as his eyes held hers, still mocking, and she forced herself to say: "And I am sure I can play this part."

Suddenly, Tor Douglas was all attention; he sat upright, his big-boned frame towering over her, intent and formidable, as his deep brown eyes seemed to take in every detail of her appearance.

"Do you know the piece?"

"It's a romantic comedy, isn't it? Set in the eighteenth century. We did Sheridan and Goldsmith at drama school—and I'm auditioning for the maidservant. I don't see why a maid shouldn't be small."

"It isn't merely that you are small, my child. You look about fourteen, and this maid, Polly, is a knowing, saucy little flirt." He smiled condescendingly. "I doubt whether you've ever really kissed a man?"

Marigold could not have disliked him more. Her anger rose, struggling with her nerves, and her voice rang with seeming confidence. "I'm twenty. And I'm an actor, so whether I've 'really kissed' a man or not doesn't matter, does it?"

I wonder how much kissing experience you had at my age, she wondered, trying to guess how old he was. *Thirty-five? Forty? No, surely not old enough to be my father.* These thoughts were unhelpful; she must concentrate!

Without taking his eyes from her face, he pushed a script across the desk to her. "Scene four. Page seventeen."

Marigold gulped. He was asking her to read at sight, unprepared!

"Don't you want to hear my audition pieces first?" she asked, quavering a little.

"Never mind your stupid pieces. Read this scene. I'll read in for Lord Harcourt."

They began. Tor read brilliantly, his deep and powerful voice filling the small office, and his strong, expressive features responding to every change of the character's moods. Marigold began hesitantly, but her enjoyment of the play soon overcame her nervousness; absorbed by the pacy tale of flirtation and intrigue, she found the character of Polly engagingly cheeky, with plenty of chances for comedy.

Marigold noticed that, though Tor read flawlessly, every time she raised her eyes from the script, his eyes were fixed on her. Occasionally, he smiled.

As they read on, Marigold saw with alarm that there was a passionate kiss toward the end of the scene. Would she be expected to kiss him right now, across the desk, at a first reading? *Too bad if I'm supposed to, I won't do it,* she decided. *I'm here to show I can act, not pass a kissing test!*

Luckily, a few lines before the embrace a knock sounded at the door, and Tor stopped reading.

"Come in," he said with controlled patience.

The door opened and a young man in paint-covered overalls came in. He unfolded a large sheet of paper covered with complicated designs and figures and laid it on the desk, looking apologetically at Tor. "Sorry to bother you, Mr. Douglas, but we've hit another problem with the set.'"

Tor groaned in a humorous way, raising his eyes to heaven. "What is it this time?"

"It's this door that Noel Marchmont wanted here, upstage right. As you can see from the plan, there's no clearance between the flat there and the dock wall here."

Marigold studied the two heads bent intently over the plan, contrasting Tor's thick, almost black, wiry locks with the unnamed stranger's floppy brown hair, speckled with white paint.

Both men were completely in their element, and respectful of each other's expertise. Tor was listening to a practical solution to the design problem with the same superb concentration he had, a minute before, been focusing on her. Finally, they lifted their heads and seemed almost surprised that Marigold was still there.

"Ah, yes. Miss Aubrey," said Tor, flashing her a smile of sudden warmth. "Meet Don Burlington, who has just saved my life again. Our stage carpenter."

Don extended a grimy hand and nodded, giving her a sympathetic smile.

"I hope we'll be seeing you back here soon, Miss Aubrey."

After Don left the room, Marigold felt her nervousness returning. Would she be expected to start the audition all over again?

Tor was leaning back in his swivel chair, hands clasped under his chin, regarding her in silence for what seemed like eternity. Finally, he spoke. "I liked some of the things you did with that scene."

Dozens of stupid questions rose to Marigold's lips, but she swallowed them back and tried to seem poised and mature. "Does that mean—you want me for the part?"

"I have some other people to see this afternoon...I've got your details, haven't I?" He rummaged among the papers on his desk and Marigold caught a glimpse of other photographs, other young hopefuls, before he held her C.V. in his large hands.

"Here we are. Marigold Aubrey. Trained at the London School of Drama—good. No professional experience whatsoever—not so good. 'Marigold Aubrey'—what on earth made you choose an old-fashioned stage name like that?"

Tor's quizzical smile held no terrors for Marigold now; she was sure she hadn't gotten the part, and she met his teasing gaze with flashing eyes. "It's the name my parents gave me, and I happen to like it."

However, she was not prepared for what happened next. Tor suddenly rose from his chair and moved swiftly round the table until he stood in front of her. He brought his face close to hers—so close that she could see herself reflected in his piercing dark brown eyes.

"You say on your C.V. that your eyes are blue," he said accusingly.

"They are blue," Marigold answered as coolly as she could under that haunting stare.

"They're not blue. They are the turquoise of the Mediterranean Sea in summer."

Abruptly, he stood back and gave her a dazzling smile.

Marigold could feel her heart thumping, but she tried to make a graceful exit. Before she reached the safety of the door, he flung out his hand, stopping her in her tracks.

"Call in at the office before you go. Carol will give you a pittance toward your expenses."

Marigold stammered her thanks and, once safely in the corridor, almost ran to a nearby open window. Leaning out she took several deep and shuddering breaths, trying not to think about the mistakes she had made in her first ever audition. If this was life in the theatre, was she up to it?

Ever since she could remember, Marigold had wanted to be an actor. As an only child, she had relieved her loneliness by dressing up and pretending to be imaginary characters as soon as she could walk and talk. Her parents, not having had any connections with the theatre, were surprised at her talent and had always been supportive—but every parent thinks their child can act. Her father, who ran a small grocery business, had little cash to spare, so Marigold was overjoyed when, in the teeth of fierce competition, she won a scholarship to the London School of Drama.

Three years as a student had trained her for the technical needs of the profession, but as to the other more demanding, personal challenges...Marigold was dreading those.

Few of the other students in her final year had found jobs—the women were having an especially hard time. Her best friend Betsy was currently working as a waitress, and Marigold expected that she would soon be joining her—unless, by some miracle, she was accepted at the Tower Theatre Company for the summer season. That would give her the chance to play in a repertory company for four months, trying out all kinds of different roles, and she would be taking the first steps in proving herself to her parents.

Marigold gazed dreamily out of the window at the winding river and the white spire of the church on the marsh plain of Branchester. It was a pretty little seaside village on the east coast, not too far from London, busy with tourists in the summer season and proud of its cultural life. Slowly she made her way to the office. There was no point in becoming too attached to the place. Probably this would be her first and last visit.

Carol Davies, the company administrator, was kind but briskly efficient. She mentioned to Marigold who the other company members were, and said that, should she be taken on for the summer season, there was a list of suitable landladies in the office. Carol even provided a timetable of trains back to London.

"Oh, and you'd better give me a contact number—not a mobile, if possible. Where will you be tonight?" she asked, just as Marigold was leaving. "Mr. Douglas doesn't believe in making people wait."

"You mean—he'll make his decision today?" Marigold gulped.

Carol smiled. "He knows how on edge you're feeling, believe me. And he's very sure of his own mind. He'll be in touch very soon."

All too soon, Marigold was out in the sunshine, slightly dazed and even more unsure about how well she had done in the interview. She decided to have a cup of coffee before heading back to Betsy's flat and the nail-biting wait for Tor's call.

The Tower Theatre was a pretty, red-brick Victorian building, built on the site of a mediaeval granary—hence the name. Parts of the old tower had been preserved and restored and it was now open to the public. As the theatre had grown larger and more successful, a new block of offices, scenery workshops, and rehearsal rooms had been constructed around a little complex of shops and a café. In the center of the precinct was a mock-Victorian fountain with some delicately leafed trees providing dappled shade.

Outside the café, tempting in the sun, were chairs and tables, and it was here Marigold sat, sipping her coffee and watching people go in and out of the theatre, wondering if any of them were also here for an audition, or if they might be members of her future audience.

*

Betsy welcomed Marigold later that evening with a warm hug and a takeaway pizza from the Italian restaurant where she worked. Her infectious optimism cheered Marigold; maybe the audition had not been quite the disaster she imagined.

"Come on—he read the whole scene with you," Betsy reminded her, "and he had a good look at you."

"Good look through me, more like," murmured Marigold, remembering those unnerving dark brown eyes. "But he didn't say if he liked me. And he didn't ask me to sing. He was rude, and he made a personal comment about me."

"Ooh, what did he say?"

"I'm not telling you! It probably didn't mean anything, I just didn't get the feeling that he liked my work."

"He was playing with you! You know what directors are like—they're power-crazed egomaniacs," said Betsy airily, and it was true that several of their student productions had been directed by professionals. But Marigold had learned today that being a drama student was light years away from the world of professional theatre.

She couldn't settle to anything, in spite of Betsy trying her best to distract her. When her phone rang at about ten o'clock that night, Marigold was too wound up to answer it herself.

"Oh, give it to me, I'm not scared of him." Betsy grabbed the phone and answered it. "Quick! You take it! It's him!"

Marigold felt her insides turn to water as she heard those deep, vibrant tones speaking her name for the second time that day. It was indeed Tor, and his voice was warm.

"Marigold—I'm inviting you to join the Tower Theatre Company. I hope very much that you'll enjoy being on our team. We start on Monday; I'll have Carol send you a script and a contract. Any questions?"

Marigold's voice, when she could find it, was squeaky with excitement. "No. That's fine. Well, it's wonderful, actually. I'm really pleased. I'm...amazed...thanks, Mr. Douglas."

She was relieved when he said a brisk goodbye and put the phone down to save her further babbling.

Betsy exploded with delight.

"You got it! Your first audition and you walked away with it! I knew you'd get it!"

They danced crazily all round the flat, giggling and hugging each other. Marigold suddenly felt as if she could do anything. She had gotten her first real job as an actor. A contract and a script! It was all too wonderful to be real.

After they stopped dancing, Betsy fetched a bottle of fizzy wine. They popped the cork and toasted each other, the Tower Theatre, success, and the future. Then Marigold gave a little shiver of excitement.

"Now what?" asked Betsy, refilling her glass.

"I've just remembered—I'm going to be acting with people like Barrie Leicester."

Betsy's eyes widened. "Barrie Leicester from *Street Life*? Why didn't you tell me that before? I've adored that man since I was sixteen! He's a celeb, big time!"

"Oh, don't! I was trying not to think about the other actors. I was so sure I hadn't got it."

"I've watched him every Tuesday and Thursday night for years—remember the episode where he got put in prison? I cried myself to sleep." Betsy sighed. "I wouldn't have thought comedy was his thing, really. I always see him in his leather jacket, snarling and being tough, but with a heart of gold."

"He can't wear a leather jacket for this—it's supposed to be eighteenth century. Oh, and there's another star. Lydia Dawlish!"

"What? *The* Lydia Dawlish, from the National? Lady Macbeth, and Nora in *A Doll's House*, and Catherine of Medici—you name it, she's been it?"

Betsy's knowledge of actors was encyclopaedic.

Marigold nodded. "There were posters with her name blazoned all over them in the office. She's a real crowd puller. I'll be terrified being on stage with her—she's got such presence."

"No you won't, you dope. When you've been through a few weeks' rehearsal together, you'll be like sisters. She'll probably become your best friend. You're one of the company now. It's an ensemble, it's democratic."

Marigold laughed. "Democratic" was not how she would have described Tor Douglas, with his uncompromising comments on her name and appearance, and the way he seemed to enjoy disconcerting her. Still—he *had* said welcome to the team.

"I bet you'll fall madly in love with Barrie," mused Betsy, but Marigold gave her a friendly shove.

"No way. It's career first, for the next five years. You know what a struggle I had to get the scholarship, and I've managed to avoid 'romance' for the past three years. I know what boys said behind my back, and it never bothered me. But now I've got my first break! I'd be crazy to let a relationship get in the way. I'm going there to work. Really hard."

Betsy gave her a quizzical look. "I'll remind you of that a month from now. No, I bet it won't even take a month. I give you a week."

"Oh wow...Monday! I start this Monday! I'm nervous already." But even as she said the words, Marigold could feel a huge grin spreading over her face. "You will come to the first night, won't you?"

"Mm, let me look in my diary—what do you think, you idiot? Of course I'll be there. Raging lions couldn't keep me away. If it was my first night and you weren't there, I'd kill you. Oh, and promise you'll introduce me to Barrie Leicester, or I'll absolutely never speak to you again."

CHAPTER TWO

At nine o'clock on Monday morning, Marigold was standing in front of the long mirror in her tiny room in Mrs. Harbour's theatrical "digs." She was wearing her lucky rehearsal clothes: green leggings, a kingfisher blue tee shirt, and blue leather jazz shoes, size four. Her wavy red-gold hair was piled on top of her head to try and give her a few extra centimeters of height. Five feet nothing, since she was fifteen! Just a few more inches was all she wanted, so directors didn't pat her on the head and suggest she played children's parts. From the mirror, her reflection stared back: a frank, roundish face, high cheekbones liberally sprinkled with freckles that were the bane of Marigold's life and which she constantly, and unsuccessfully, hoped would fade with time, a small tilted nose, and a generous mouth that widened to a ready smile. Her teeth, she had been told, were one of her best features, being perfectly regular and white, but her eyes also had a fascinating, full-lashed intensity that made it hard to look away. *Is this the face of a future famous actor?* she asked herself a little uncertainly.

No time to sing Maria's song from *The Sound of Music* to boost up her spirits—it was time to go.

What little confidence she had began to ebb away as soon as she came in sight of the Victorian façade of the Tower Theatre. In the late May sunlight, the red brick glowed softly and the grey flint of the old tower pointed heavenward like an exclamation mark.

Since her audition, the sign painters had been at work advertising the eight plays that would be performed by the regular company from June to September, and there was also a full list of the company members, in alphabetical order. Marigold giggled nervously as she noticed that her name appeared first, before those of Barrie Leicester and Lydia Dawlish!

She made her way round the side of the theatre to the stage door and began climbing the stone steps to Rehearsal Room One on the top floor. Thanks to Carol Davies's helpful advice, she knew they would be rehearsing here for the first week, before moving downstairs to the real theatre. A week after this play opened, they would begin rehearsing the next one during the day, while continuing to perform every night. It was a full schedule, but Marigold welcomed the challenge, hoping she would be given a good range of parts to make her professional debut one to be noticed.

She pushed open the swing doors and walked in, trying to ignore the sudden thudding of her heart.

The room was wide and airy, with huge windows that looked out onto the sea. At one end was an enormous mirror with a practice barre that ran the length of the wall. Marigold noticed with pleasure that the floor was tiled in springy vinyl rubber—easy to dance on and warm enough to roll about on. She wondered if anyone else was accustomed to doing the vigorous warm-up exercises that her teachers at drama school had told her were essential to a good performance.

At the far end of the room was an old upright piano, and around it were grouped several people, laughing and chatting like old friends. Marigold took a deep breath and walked quickly up to them. They all turned to look at her with the polite curiosity actors always have for one of their own kind. She smiled back.

"I'm Marigold Aubrey—hello, everyone."

After a momentary silence, one of the group came toward her with a brilliant smile of welcome. "Hi, Marigold. You look lovely. My name's—"

But there was no need for Barrie Leicester to introduce himself. She recognized him immediately. She felt her hand being pressed in a warm grip, and then he pulled her gently toward him and briefly encircled her with one arm. She was being embraced by Barrie Leicester!

In the flesh he looked a little older than the twenty-something boy he seemed on television, but the famous blue eyes and blonde curls were every bit as authentic and engaging. His voice, boyish and husky, was the one that had sent shivers down so many schoolgirls' spines.

Barrie's welcome broke the ice, and then everyone came forward, shaking hands, kissing her, and introducing themselves. Marigold noticed that Tor was not there. Nor was Lydia Dawlish.

"Tor will arrive on the dot of ten," Barrie told her, "and work will begin as soon as he steps through that swing door, so be on your toes ready to go."

"And Lydia will glide in at five past, and woe betide anyone who comments on that," said a rather plump woman who had introduced herself as Helen Grant.

An elderly, nearly bald man with wobbly jowls and gold-rimmed spectacles gazed anxiously at Marigold. He was holding a paper cup of coffee. "My goodness, darling, you look ready for a marathon," he murmured. "You're not going to make us all jog on the spot, are you?"

Before Marigold could answer, the door opened and Tor Douglas strode in, as promptly as Barrie had predicted. But Helen was wrong, for on his heels came Lydia Dawlish.

Marigold saw at once that she was tall—nearly as tall as Tor himself—pencil-slim, and very, very beautiful. A cascade of wavy black hair rippled almost to her waist, and the arch of her eyebrows looked like the work of some exquisite painter. Her mouth was an impossibly perfect cupid's bow, and her eyes were so dark they looked almost black. Not a blemish or a wrinkle marred her complexion—it was impossible to tell her age from her appearance. Yet Marigold knew that Lydia's starry career had begun at least ten years ago, while she, Marigold, was still a pigtailed schoolgirl.

Marigold stared so long at this vision that before she had realized it, everyone else had picked up a chair and was sitting in a circle around Tor. Blushing with embarrassment, she joined them. Tor put down a large notebook on the floor beside him and his gaze traveled slowly around the seven members of the company. He made a short and witty welcoming speech, smiling warmly at each of them, and invited them to introduce themselves. With a courtly gesture he turned first to Lydia, who was sitting next to him.

"I am Lydia Dawlish, delighted to be back here for another season. Playing Lady Sophie."

That was all she said, but it was enough for Marigold to realize how far she herself had to go in experience, technique, and concentration. Lydia was a class act; she made you watch her every move and she caressed you with the velvety tones of her unforgettable voice.

"I'm Brian Hancock, playing the judge and various assorted butlers and constables—and washing Tor's socks, if asked," said the elderly man, and his words won a ripple of laughter from the group. He made a funny face at Marigold, and a little half-bow in Tor's direction.

Marigold wished she was able to relax like him, and make jokes about their director. She realized she had put her chair as far away from Tor as she could.

"Barrie Leicester. Lord Harcourt." He flashed a smile at Marigold, and her heart skipped as beat as she thought ahead to the love scenes she would play with him, including the one she had read at the audition with Tor. *What will Betsy say*, she thought to herself, *when I tell her I'm kissing Barrie Leicester several times a day!* Her face broke into a broad smile as she introduced herself:

"I'm Marigold Aubrey, playing the maid, Polly."

"My name is Helen Grant and I play Melissa, Lady Sophie's confidante."

Marigold wondered if these two were suited to play each other's friends. Helen seemed rather subdued and had a ferrety smile, but Lydia nodded in a gracious way that made her seem kindly and approachable. Maybe Betsy was right—Lydia was probably a lovely person, in spite of her celebrity status.

"Robin Cooper, playing the footman and understudying Lord Harcourt." Robin was a lively, brown-haired young man only a few years older than Marigold, dressed in jeans and a sweatshirt. He gave her a friendly grin and a wink.

"Evelyn de Laurier, playing Lady Trensham, Lady Sophie's grandmother." Why were the old lady's hands trembling as she spoke?

As she looked into those watery blue eyes, Marigold was surprised to see her own nervousness reflected in them. Her friendly smile was returned by the old lady, but rather shakily.

On Tor's left was a blonde girl about Marigold's age who had not yet spoken. She was burdened with a clipboard, several copies of the script, a stopwatch, and a notebook. At Tor's invitation she mumbled, staring at the floor, "Jenny Warren, assistant stage manager for the company."

Introductions over, Tor went straight into a full read-through of the play. It was called *The Reluctant Rake,* and though it ended happily, it offered enough high drama, farce, and romance to satisfy the most demanding audience.

Even though she already knew the script from reading it through several times a day since it had arrived, Marigold was enchanted to hear how the play came to life in the hands of this experienced professional cast. How easy it was to laugh at the jokes and weep real tears in the tragic scenes. Toward the end of the play, Lydia read her long and moving speech so exquisitely that they all gave her spontaneous applause, and she appeared to come out of a dream as she acknowledged them all, her dark eyes huge with tears.

At the end of the read-through they broke for coffee, and Marigold felt her shyness melting away as the cast sought her out, asked her a few questions, and plied her with information about themselves. She was by far the youngest and most inexperienced, but, as Betsy had said, they all seemed determined to put her at her ease.

Only Lydia and Tor remained at a distance. Lydia disappeared from the room, saying she was "gasping for a fag."

Tor had already given them all a strict note about the absolute ban on smoking in the rehearsal room. He was absorbed in conversation with Jenny Warren throughout the break. She took notes and nodded vigorously. Marigold breathed a sigh of relief that her job did not involve such close proximity to Tor. It looked as if Jenny was as scared of him as she was herself.

When the break was over, Tor asked if there were any questions, and listened patiently and attentively to queries about time off, rehearsal hours, whether agents would be invited to the first night, and how many of the London papers would be attending. Marigold caught her breath as Tor casually mentioned the journalists who usually reviewed Tower Theatre productions. Finally, the questions died away and Marigold, feeling as if she was at school, put her hand up to attract Tor's attention.

"Yes, Marigold?" His unnerving gaze was fixed on her with full concentration, and she found it just as disconcerting as she had at the audition.

"Two things. Will you be leading us in a warm up before rehearsals? You know, for voice and movement?"

Her innocent question caused a ripple of not entirely friendly laughter around the group. Brian Hancock pretended to stagger and faint, Lydia murmured something in a husky undertone to Helen Grant, who was sitting next to her, and they both smiled ironically in Tor's direction.

Tor, on the other hand, took her question entirely seriously, and nodded briefly before answering. "I see the London School of Drama still trains its students as thoroughly as ever. However, I shall be unable to lead a warm-up as I have meetings until ten each morning and rehearsal time is extremely tight—more so once the season has begun. So—" he briefly conferred with Jenny "—Jenny will arrange for this room to be open and available at half-past nine for anyone who wishes to limber up before we start, so you'll have half an hour before we begin each morning. Does that seem okay?" His reassuring glance gave Marigold the courage to ask her second question.

"I was wondering why we are rehearsing up here, when we have an empty theatre downstairs. Wouldn't it save time to begin blocking the scenes on the proper stage?"

This question was not received quite so kindly. There were snorts of laughter and giggles from the other actors, and Tor answered shortly, "Of course it would save a great deal of time. But has it not occurred to you that we are not the only people involved with this production? While we are rehearsing up here, Don Burlington and his stage crew are working with the designer on building and painting the set, the lights are being rigged, the electricians are running cables everywhere and the stage is like Piccadilly Circus."

What a stupid mistake! Of course she knew that, but in her nervousness she had forgotten everything about theatre production she had been taught.

"I'm sorry—I didn't think—" she stammered, her face scarlet. Tor was standing up, having already dismissed her from his thoughts. Marigold hated herself for this elementary blunder, and Tor for the way he had put her down. It was a relief to feel a friendly hand squeezing hers as they began the blocking rehearsal, and to hear Barrie's voice in her ear:

"Don't worry about him, he's a grouchy old bear. We'll start rehearsing onstage next week. Now, cheer up; you were splendid at the read-through."

Gratefully, she flashed him a wobbly smile.

Blocking rehearsals were tiring and needed all of Marigold's concentration. Jenny Warren had marked the exact shape and size of the stage on the floor with white tape, while the main pieces of scenery—the "flats"—were marked in red. There were taped outlines of every single piece of furniture, some of which would be hired and some built in the theatre workshops, and Marigold had to remember not to walk over chairs and tables as she scurried around the set, opening imaginary doors and picking up imaginary cloaks and fans.

Tor had already planned all the moves, and every player wrote each of theirs down next to the line of dialogue that went with it. It wasn't as exciting as the read-through because everyone rattled off the lines expressionlessly, writing down their moves and any "business" they would need to learn.

By lunchtime, they had blocked the first four scenes, and Marigold was desperate for a break. She saw Brian, Lydia, and Helen go off together, Robin scoot off on his racing bike, Evelyn resting on an old leather chaise longue with a chiffon scarf over her face, and Tor and Jenny, still chatting and going up to the office, presumably.

Marigold was beginning to feel a bit lost when Barrie came up behind her, seized her hand, and pulled her along with him through the swing doors and down the stairs. "Come on, Goldie—lunchtime is crucial for the energy. Let's join the gang."

They arrived at the café in the little square and were soon sitting with the other actors at one of the sunny tables, crunching baguettes and drinking coffee. Barrie sat down opposite her, attacking his baguette in between talking to everyone about everything that had happened since they were together last season.

Marigold was dying to ask him questions about the television series that had made him famous, but she felt she would appear such a silly schoolgirl that she just smiled and listened as he chatted.

"We've got some rather fruity scenes together, haven't we?" he said, grinning disarmingly. "It would be helpful to get to know each other a little outside of work, don't you think? There's a crowd of us meeting later on for drinks in the 'Lord Nelson'—the big pub down on the sea front. How about meeting me there at eight thirty?" Hardly pausing to acknowledge Marigold's shy nod, he went on easily, "Oh, and don't get scared of Tor, even when he bites your head off, which he will. He only does it to make us all sit up. He's an old pussycat when you get to know him."

Marigold shook her head. "I don't want to get to know him. As long as I can get through rehearsals without being made to feel small—smaller than I am already, if that's possible—I'll be fine."

Barrie's eyes twinkled as he answered, "I think your size is perfect. When we kiss onstage, you'll have to stand on tiptoe and the audience will just adore it."

"Oh—the audience! I'd forgotten all about them!"

Barrie looked very serious for a moment. Then he gently took her hand and gave it a friendly squeeze. "Never, never forget them, my sweet. First rule of theatre."

Brian Hancock, sitting next to him, launched into a funny anecdote about the worst audience he had ever known, and this was capped by Lydia and Helen, until the whole table rang with laughter, and passers-by, noticing who they were, stopped and stared.

Marigold tried to look as if she was used to this attention. A girl her own age came up and asked Barrie for his autograph. A year ago, that girl could have been her.

Rehearsal ended at six o'clock, and by then they had blocked about half of the play. Marigold was tired, and looking forward to going back to her room, having a cup of tea and something to eat, and doing some intensive work on her script.

As she was leaving, Tor Douglas strolled over to her. "Nice work today, Marigold. Keep it up." He looked at her with his keen eyes. "I don't suppose you know anyone in Branchester, do you?"

"No—well, only the other actors."

He looked at his watch. "There are some lovely old pubs here. Would you like to come for a drink later on?"

His large, unnerving dark eyes were still fixed on hers, and Marigold realized that for once he was unaccompanied by Jenny Warren. No one else was in the room.

"I'm sorry. I can't tonight. I'm going out with—er—well, anyway, I have to get home and change and—"

With a wave of his hand, Tor conveyed that he was not interested in what she had to say. "Another time, perhaps." It was a statement, not a question, and as soon as he had spoken he seemed to lose interest in her; he opened his notebook and began writing.

Marigold knew she had been dismissed, but something made her refuse to accept it. She was an adult. This was not a school. She waited until he looked up from his book again, and then said, "What about tomorrow?"

She was slightly surprised at her own daring, but he only frowned.

"Tomorrow's no good."

He was gone before she could say another word, and Marigold felt relieved; the idea of going for a drink alone with this man was scary. She picked up her script and left the room.

After she had coaxed the plumbing in Mrs. Harbour's antiquated bathroom to deliver enough hot water for a reluctant shower, she looked through her minimal wardrobe for something to wear. She had no idea who Barrie would be introducing her to, but surely he would not expect her to dress up?

"Too bad if he does, because I haven't got anything glamorous here—only my first night outfit, and I have to save that. If he'd wanted arm candy, he should have asked Lydia."

She put on a simple blue summer dress with a narrow waist and a full skirt, and a short satin jacket, pale grey with blue embroidery, that she had found in Camden Lock market. Her shoe department was sadly deficient; when she was a student she had spent any spare money on practice shoes, but she had one pair of silver sandals with thin leather straps, and they would have to do.

Surveying herself critically in the mirror, she wished again for a few extra inches in height and sighed as she saw how the June sunshine had brought out even more freckles. It was no use trying to cover them with makeup—the only kind that was thick enough was stage makeup, and that looked ridiculous under ordinary light, so she made do with some pale pink lipstick and a dusting of powder.

When she was finally ready, she went to find Mrs. Harbour in her downstairs parlor.

She was knitting at a shapeless garment of indeterminate hue, with much clicking of needles. All around her on the brightly patterned wallpaper of her best room were photographs of celebrities: actors, singers, musicians, all signed with personal dedications to herself or her late husband, Herbert.

Marigold was greeted with a cheery welcome as Mrs. Harbour patted the cushion of the chair next to her with a plump hand.

"And where are you off to?"

"Just to the Lord Nelson with Barrie and some friends."

Mrs. Harbour smiled and nodded without dropping a stitch.

"Has he stayed here?"

Mrs. Harbour pointed with her knitting needle at a small photo of a much younger Barrie. "Oh, bless you, yes, of course he has. That picture was from his first season at the Tower—let me think—eight years ago? He has his own place now—a very nice penthouse on the seafront."

"Is he—married?" inquired Marigold casually.

Mrs. Harbour fiddled with a tricky purling maneuver. "Can't say for sure—but I don't think so. Not the marrying kind, is

Barrie. Not like poor Mr. Douglas." Mrs Harbour sighed in a tantalizing way.

Marigold suddenly felt herself blushing, and at the same time, she was seized with curiosity. It would be nice to hear something about Tor that made him seem more human and fallible. What did she mean, "Poor Mr. Douglas"?

"Did he ever stay with you?"

Mrs. Harbour looked at Marigold over her spectacles. "No, he's never been one of my gentlemen. But there was a lot about it in the papers, you know the kind of thing."

Marigold didn't know. She was dying to ask, but at that moment one of Mrs. Harbour's other lodgers came in with some question about cinemas, and Marigold realized her opportunity was gone. She asked for directions to the pub, and was given the same street map Carol Davies had already given her.

Walking along the quiet streets, Marigold wished her mind could remain more firmly on the play and less on the personalities of the company. The image of Tor's dark-browed face suddenly rose before her—she did not look forward with any pleasure to another day of that deep voice and critical gaze. Then there was the divine Lydia, who so far had seemed completely oblivious to Marigold's existence, and the worrying sidelong glances and comments of Helen Grant. Still, she felt she had a potential friend and ally in Barrie.

As she entered the lounge of the pub, she saw that famous curly head amid a sea of unfamiliar faces. Barrie waved her over and gestured to an empty chair near him.

"What can I get you?" he asked, and several wags immediately stuck their empty glasses under his nose. "How about some wine?"

"Thanks, that would be lovely. Dry white, please." As Barrie disappeared in the direction of the bar, Marigold saw that she was not the only member of the Tower Theatre company here. Helen Grant was nursing a tomato juice, and on a small stool beside her was Jenny Warren, her head bent. Marigold went and sat next to them, and was rewarded with a shy smile from Jenny.

"How are you feeling after your first day?" asked Helen. It seemed a friendly question, yet Marigold sensed a subtext hidden underneath her words.

Luckily, Barrie returned then with drinks, and interrupted the conversation with his usual ebullience, introducing Marigold to four or five men in swift succession. "This is the gorgeous girl I get to kiss in the line of business," he announced, resting his hand briefly on top of Marigold's head. Smiles greeted this, which made her feel awkward and irritated.

"How's Tor behaving these days?" someone asked, and Barrie turned to Marigold.

"What would you say, darling—is he a tiger or a pussycat? Or a lovable old moggy, with the occasional flash of sabre-tooth?"

Much as she disliked the man, Marigold felt disloyal discussing Tor in this gathering, and looked for help to Jenny Warren, but she was only staring at Barrie with open admiration, while Helen Grant's mouth was curled in a small and secret smile. Marigold looked around her at their expectant faces and challenged Barrie—with humor, she hoped. "Is that a fair question?"

Barrie shrugged and made a comic face.

"I mean, he's not here to answer, so why say things behind his back?"

"Love-fifteen to the redhead," murmured someone behind her, and Barrie made a dismissive gesture.

"Ah, forget it, it was only a bit of fun."

One of the men introduced himself as Dave West and offered Marigold some pork scratchings, which she refused, feeling less and less like socializing.

"We've all worked with Tor," Dave said, kindly enough, "and of course, you don't know anything about him or his background, but working with him can be heaven. Or hell. And that's bound to have an effect on the success of the season."

"He's an excellent director," answered Marigold, but stopped when she caught Barrie looking at her with raised eyebrows. Was he trying to make her look stupid? What did she actually know about directors?

Luckily, the conversation moved on, as someone else's reputation was held up for scrutiny. It was no one Marigold knew, and she went and sat with Jenny, hoping to find some common ground.

"I'm not enjoying this—are you?" she whispered to Jenny, whose fair hair swung over her face as she bent her head over her drink. Her shyness in this group made it impossible for her to get a word in edgeways.

"They—they don't mean any of it," she stammered. "It's how actors talk all the time. Barrie isn't mean, really he isn't."

Marigold could not help gazing at those famous features as Barrie animatedly led the conversation, which had moved on to the subject of fast cars.

He was, she could see, conventionally handsome, with his abundant curly fair hair, those eloquent eyes, his regular features, and slightly tanned fair skin. There were fascinating little wrinkles at the corners of his wide blue eyes, but in spite of his maturity there was something about the set of his mouth—a rather weak mouth, she noticed—that reminded her of a spoiled little boy.

His generosity was not in question, however, for he would not let her buy any drinks and supplied not only herself, but Jenny and Helen, too.

Marigold refused a third glass of wine.

"I daren't risk a hangover! Think how angry Tor would be."

A queer expression flitted across Barrie's face as he gave Helen a cigarette, but all he said was, "And we mustn't upset Tor, must we?"

That was enough to make Marigold leave, having said a polite round of goodbyes.

To her surprise, as she hit the street, Barrie was behind her, catching up with her and taking her arm.

"Goldie—wait! Please, don't go yet. I was being insufferable. And what an appalling bunch of dreadful people—I know, I could see you were hating it. Please, Goldie, stay just another ten minutes?"

"I can't. I really don't want to—" Marigold pulled her arm away, feeling suddenly exhausted, but as she turned, Barrie blocked her way, looking determined.

She spun round, intending to go the other way—and bumped straight into Tor Douglas.

He took in the situation at a glance, and moved aside to let Marigold pass. She could not meet his eyes as he walked on without a word.

"Barrie, please let me go home. What must Tor have thought?"

"I don't give a toss what he thinks. I'd like to walk you home—that's all."

"I'm tired."

"I'll give you a lift."

"Thanks, I'd rather walk."

He fell into step beside her, and Marigold wondered how much better Betsy would have handled this situation. Barrie's earlier talkative mood seemed to have evaporated and he was lost in thought for a while. When he eventually looked at her, he was apologetic and altogether charming again.

"I'm sorry. This evening went pear-shaped. You were absolutely right to pull me up. Tor is a fine director—we couldn't wish for a better." He flashed her an uncertain, boyish smile. "I do hope we're still friends?"

"It started off wrong because of the way you introduced me to your crowd," Marigold said.

He looked surprised, then contrite. "Oh, the 'gorgeous girl I get to kiss' routine? You are so right, it was unforgivable—Barrie Leicester at his worst, living up to his *Street Life* reputation. The trouble is, people expect you to have an amazing romantic life if you're as successful as I am. They all think I only have to wave my little finger and beautiful young women will come running. And of course, it's a load of cobblers."

He grinned disarmingly, then stopped and lit a cigarette. "Is this making sense, or does it sound like I'm trying to wriggle my way out of the truth? I forget, until I meet a genuine person like you, how shallow most showbiz people are. What saddens me is that real love maybe only comes once in a lifetime. And when I had my chance, I threw it away."

He stopped walking and drew deeply on his cigarette.

Marigold saw how perfectly his gestures belonged to the world of TV close-ups. Dead on cue, Barrie tossed the half-smoked cigarette away and shoved his hands in his pockets, smiling bravely into the distance.

"There was a girl, Lindy...she left me, just before I got my break in *Street Life*. I really, truly loved her. With all my foolish heart. And she left me over a silly row and I have never stopped regretting it."

"Was she an actor?"

"She could have been, but she wasn't ruthless enough. She expected the world to be nice to her. I tried as hard as I could to help her, but in the end, she gave me an ultimatum."

"What did she say?"

"That I had to give up the *Street Life* audition and—oh, I'm not going to go there. I couldn't do it. She moved out the next day and I never saw her again."

Barrie's eyes filled with tears—real tears. His voice was shaking. Marigold felt her own eyes growing moist. His grief was genuine—had to be genuine. And he was sharing this deeply personal moment just with her.

"The saddest thing was, I could have been so happy with her. I think I'm basically a domestic sort of person, you know—kids, a dog, a bit of DIY at weekends. I'm just an ordinary guy under it all. I long for security, in a business as rocky as ours."

"You sound as if you've made your mind up that it will never happen," said Marigold gently. She decided she did like him, after all.

"I haven't given up hope completely. It's just that nice people are very thin on the ground."

Marigold said with great certainty, "Well, I'm not looking for security. I would hate to be settled down with kids and a dog."

He answered her softly, "I'd wait a long time for the right girl."

As they turned down Marigold's street, she thought what a strange mixture Barrie was. Completely charming one minute, adorably vulnerable the next, and transparently self-absorbed a moment later.

"There you go, Goldilocks," he said, depositing her on Mrs. Harbour's doorstep, "and try not to hate me too much after what happened tonight."

"I don't make judgments like that on the spur of the moment," she answered.

But later, lying in the narrow single bed, she realized she had done exactly that, in the case of Tor Douglas.

CHAPTER THREE

Promptly at half past nine the next morning, Marigold pulled open the doors to the rehearsal room. She was not expecting to see anyone else there, and she welcomed the chance to be alone. She put down her bag, removed her cardigan, and began her warm-up exercises. Her night out and two glasses of wine had not affected her too much.

Her warm-up was disturbed by the door opening as Robin Cooper appeared, minus his bike.

"Hi. Thought you were so brave yesterday. I wanted to ask about warm-ups but I lost my nerve. Oh, don't let me disturb you."

Marigold noticed that Robin was beginning a series of balletic movements that required extreme flexibility and strength. They worked in silence for five minutes or so, then the door swung open again and, to Marigold's amazement, Helen Grant appeared, looking rather diffident. She stood watching Robin for a moment, then seemed to make up her mind and came close to Marigold.

"Do you mind if I join you?"

"No, not at all." Marigold tried her hardest to be friendly, though she could not help remembering Helen's supercilious smile when the subject of warm-ups had been raised yesterday.

"The thing is, I've been trying to lose weight, and I thought, maybe a bit of exercise..."

"Great idea, Helen."

But Helen didn't seem able to start. She took off her jacket and stood looking at them both, rather helplessly. Marigold went on with her workout.

"Marigold," Helen said. "I hope you don't mind me asking—but, well, it's been ages since I did this sort of thing, and what you're doing looks good. Do you mind if I copy you?"

This was the first time Helen had shown any vulnerability; maybe they could become friends, thought Marigold. They would have to get on, as she already knew they would be sharing a dressing room. Maybe there was a nice side to Helen.

"Oh, of course you can. I'm not as advanced as Robin; this is just for basic flexibility and stretch."

Helen nodded, and they worked together. It felt good to get out of breath, and after their muscles were warmed up, they all did some voice exercises.

"We'll have a go at the ballet stuff tomorrow," Marigold said. "Robin can show us how to wrap our legs round our necks."

Helen laughed for the first time, her face relaxed and rosy. "I'm not insured for self-inflicted injuries."

When the other actors arrived, Barrie seemed to seek out Marigold for a special smile. He did not refer to the previous evening, but before she had a chance to say anything to him, Tor arrived, and serious work began.

It did not take long for the company to realize that Tor was in a vile temper. Where yesterday he had been patient and welcoming, today he was inclined to shout in his enormous voice at the least little setback. Jenny Warren was kept scurrying around obeying his bellowed orders like a frightened rabbit. Even Lydia, having opened her mouth once or twice to argue with him, thought the better of it and shut it again.

Marigold soon found out that she needed every ounce of her concentration to avoid his wrath. As it was, she forgot one of her exits and had to stand meekly with her head bowed as he roared at her.

"Have you actually got a memory in that head of yours? If you have, kindly switch it on."

Marigold was saved from tears by seeing the rest of the cast made to suffer equally from his bad temper, mostly through no fault of their own.

Things came to a horrible climax when Evelyn de Laurier, who had forgotten everything they did the day before, suddenly sank down in a chair and began weeping.

"I'm so sorry," she kept saying. "Everything's so fast. I don't seem to be able to keep up."

Tor stopped the rehearsal and ordered an early coffee break.

Evelyn confessed to everyone in a trembling voice that she had forgotten to bring her spectacles with her that morning and, so great was her terror of seeming incompetent, she had not dared to tell Tor that today she was unable to read the moves she had carefully written down the day before. As he heard her sad little story, Tor's expression changed. His brows lost their thunderous, craggy expression of rage, and he gently put his arm around the old lady.

"You really must not be afraid to tell me when there is something wrong," he said.

Robin offered immediately to go on his bike to fetch the glasses, and while he was gone, Marigold noticed how Tor, busy as he was, made Evelyn a hot drink, took it to her, and quietly engaged her in conversation until she felt able to continue.

Once Evelyn had her spectacles, her attention and concentration was fully restored, and Tor was careful not to shout at her. The rest of the company, however, still had to endure the rough edge of his tongue until lunchtime.

The trials they had been through that morning seemed to bring the whole company together, and by common consent, they all went to the café in a group, including Jenny. Tor asked her to bring him a sandwich, as he had to stay in the office and make phone calls, which relieved everyone, as the thought of sitting through the lunch break with him in that mood was unbearable.

"So, what's up with the boss?" Barrie asked Jenny as they took their places at their favorite table.

"He's a bit stressed."

"A bit stressed!" echoed Barrie, rolling his eyes.

"We had a rather difficult meeting with Noel this morning—he's gone way over budget."

Noel Marchmont was the designer, whom Marigold had already heard described as "a bit of a feather duster." She had not met him, and probably would not until they began working in the theatre and using the proper set.

"It seems that Noel made a lot of mistakes in his original drawings, and he was kind of relying on Don to help him sort them all out. At the meeting this morning, Tor made a throwaway comment that we should have used Don as designer right from the start, which would have saved loads of time and money. Noel blew his top—well, you know him, he's a really famous designer, he's worked in America and London—but Don knows how much adapting his designs need to make them work. Tor more or less said to Noel's face that other people have been covering for him. He's gotten complacent, and that's made him sloppy—and you know how angry Tor gets with incompetence."

Jenny stirred her tea vigorously, and Marigold felt a surge of admiration for this timid girl who seemed unafraid of Tor and his moods.

"How's his drinking these days?"

It was Barrie who asked the question, casually enough, but the whole table fell silent as they waited for her answer.

Jenny hesitated. *She's protecting him*, thought Marigold, *she doesn't want Tor to lose face.* What power did he have over her, to inspire such loyalty?

Finally, she said, "He's got problems, but they're nothing to do with drink. He's under a load of stress at the moment—not just the job. Other stuff—you know."

Half the group seemed to understand what she was saying, and nodded wisely. Marigold, who knew nothing about Tor's stuff, whatever it was, felt uneasy hearing things about him when he wasn't there; it seemed cowardly and mean-spirited.

Lydia blew a long exhalation of cigarette smoke. "Of course. Blanche! She was always vindictive. She's probably screwing him for every penny he earns."

Then Brian chimed in, "Oh, not just Blanche, what about number two and number one? They all want a slice of the cake."

Jenny left to buy Tor's sandwich, and the group seemed to relax a little, almost as if she was Tor's spy.

Helen Grant took up the story. "I knew his first wife. Janette Taylor—she looked a little bit like you—" Helen nodded at Marigold "—small and intense. Blonde hair. She fell madly in love with him, and he didn't suspect a thing for ages. We were working on a play for eight weeks, and there she was, pining away, while he seemed not to notice her. Then, almost on the last night, he pounced. He proposed to her in the dressing room. She said yes, of course, and they had a big showbiz wedding as soon as the play ended." Helen stubbed out her cigarette. "It lasted less than a year."

"Oh, he's impossible to live with," said Lydia. "She did the sensible thing and ran off with someone less...charismatic."

Was she speaking from personal experience? wondered Marigold. *Had she tried to live with him?*

"There was another woman that he was involved with, but she had the sense not to marry him," said Helen.

Brian was just finishing a large cream cake, and wiped his mouth on his napkin before adding his contribution. "I liked the one who wasn't in the theatre—you know, the lawyer?"

"Poor Tor," said Lydia. "It must be so difficult being pursued by gorgeous angry women wherever he goes."

Brian rolled his eyes. "Tell me about it, darling!"

A ripple of amusement ended the lunch break. It was time to begin serious work again.

That afternoon was one of the hardest of Marigold's life. As the maid, she was always running about the stage, but this afternoon

Tor seemed to take a particular delight in making her stop, go back, and run all over again.

It wasn't until the end of the afternoon tea break that she came face to face with Barrie. He was standing by the window, looking out over the sea, when she came up to him with her tea. He turned to face her, looking slightly amused.

"I believe I was a bit of a pain last night."

In the bright sunlight, she noticed how tense his mouth was. "Oh, forget it, Barrie. I wasn't feeling very sociable."

"Will you come out to dinner with me at the weekend?"

Marigold shook her head. "I don't think that's a good idea."

His mouth took on the sulky, pouting look of a disappointed small boy, and he seemed about to argue, when Tor's voice made them both jump.

"What are you two doing, standing gazing at each other when everyone else is ready to work? Tea break finished five minutes ago."

Marigold ran back to her position, and Barrie put down his cup and picked up his script without further conversation.

By five o'clock, Marigold was quietly congratulating herself on having safely navigated the treacherous rapids of Tor's moods. She even managed to get a smile of approval for one scene.

But then the heavens opened.

It began innocently enough, with a scene where Polly, who has truly fallen in love with the fickle Lord Harcourt, finds a love letter to Lady Sophie and jealously tears it up. Lady Sophie enters and, suspecting Polly of meddling in her bureau, accuses her of dishonesty. Torn between her love for Lord Harcourt and her fear of being dismissed, Polly remains silent, and Lady Sophie dismisses her. Polly, heartbroken, leaves the room.

Marigold knew that this was one of Polly's most important scenes; usually the focus of attention was the glamorous Lady Sophie, but here, the interest of the audience would briefly be on her. She had not intended to steal the scene or grab Lady Sophie's limelight, but it felt right to her that, just before making her exit, Polly should turn and look sorrowfully at her.

They ran through the scene twice, then Lydia stopped and spoke apologetically to Tor. "There's something throwing me, just here," and she pointed to Polly's exit line, "something seems to be taking an awfully long time."

Tor looked at the script, frowned, and nodded. "Cut the pause, Polly," he demanded curtly.

Marigold could hardly believe her ears. Her part was so small compared with Lydia's—surely no one could begrudge her a little attention in this scene?

"Excuse me," she addressed both Tor and Lydia. "I think the pause is needed there. Polly would pause; she's just had a terrible shock, you see, and—"

She was interrupted by a bellow of rage from Tor. "When I need an actor to tell me how to direct, I'll ask for your opinion. Until then, do as I say."

Marigold began to tremble as, transfixed by his passionate dark eyes, she felt the full power of his authority.

Lydia was staring at her with amusement, as if she was a dog walking on its hind legs.

Marigold felt furious and tearful at the same time. Furious that her best scene was being snatched away, and tearful at how powerless she was against these two giants of the profession. She had to make one more try.

"Couldn't I split the difference—have half a pause there?"

With a shout that made everyone in the room jump, Tor flung his script across the room, aimed directly at her head. It fell apart and fluttered to the ground before it reached her, and Marigold stood ready to dodge any other missiles he might want to throw. But worse was to come.

He strode toward her, eyes blazing, while Jenny scrabbled about on the floor collecting pieces of paper and reassembling the script. Tor's hand descended heavily on Marigold's shoulder, and she felt the intensity of his fury, directed entirely at her. Her insides turned to water and she could barely meet his look.

"What did you say?" he asked in a furious whisper that was more frightening than his shouts had been.

Marigold mumbled, "I asked if I could have a—a tiny pause there?"

His hand, clamped on her shoulder, tightened till it almost hurt. "No. You may not. And if you won't do as I ask, I'll find another actor who will."

Marigold, defeated, dropped her eyes.

"Now. Cut the pause, and we will continue."

He went back to his chair and Jenny handed him his script.

Marigold was furious. He was a tyrant, a despot, a bossy, overbearing beast of a man—but she had to do as he said. She continued with the scene as directed—but for her, her best scene was ruined.

At the end of the day, the cast, subdued and weary, left the rehearsal room in ones and twos. Marigold, feeling shaky, was putting her stuff away when Barrie came up to her and gave her a friendly hug.

"Still in one piece?"

"Just about."

He let her go and asked casually, "Need a lift home?"

"No thanks. I'd rather walk."

Barrie made a comic little bow. "Very well, my lady."

As soon as she was alone, Marigold felt drained of all her energy, and totally lacking in enthusiasm for the play she had cared so passionately about yesterday. As she slowly walked toward the door, she saw that Tor was blocking her way, and her heart sank.

"Marigold. I'd like you to come with me."

It was useless to protest that she was exhausted, that work was over for the day, that she did not want to spend one moment more in his presence. He led the way downstairs and along the corridor to a heavy fire door. He opened it to let her pass. As she did, their eyes met and he stopped abruptly.

"I know what you're thinking. You're thinking you can't stand the sight of me, even for five more minutes."

He had hit the nail so precisely on the head that Marigold could not help grinning. Disarmingly, he grinned right back at her.

"An understandable reaction. Don't lose any sleep over it—I won't."

And he was off, striding along the corridor so fast she had to run to keep up with him.

"I want you to see something. You're single-minded about the character you play, and you have concentration and a disciplined approach to your work, and that's all good. But you show your inexperience in your ignorance of all the things that make up this theatre, this company, this production. The building, the stage crew, the people behind the scenes—all of them are vital, just as important as you or me. It's an object lesson in humility."

Another moment and they had turned the corner into a passage that led backstage into the theatre itself. Apart from a brief glimpse on the day of her audition, Marigold had not set foot inside the theatre since she had begun working there.

Although it was past six o'clock, the place was buzzing with activity. Marigold recognized Don Burlington, the theatre carpenter who had interrupted her audition, perched high up on a gantry with two other men, lifting a heavy piece of scenery into position under a grid where it would have the ropes and pulleys attached that would enable it to be "flown" up into the roof, or flies, high above the stage.

About six men were manhandling the three main walls of the set representing Lady Sophie's drawing room, as yet unpainted wood, into a position where they could be fixed on their marks on stage. Another group was talking on their mobiles to each other as they moved lights around on the battens, or scaffold poles, running horizontally above the stage.

It was a scene of seeming confusion and noisy chaos, yet it was incredibly productive and organized. Everyone was working toward the same end, everyone understood their part in the pattern. Marigold's tiredness left her as she watched and drank it all in. Suddenly Carol Davies was at Tor's elbow.

"Ah, there you are, dear man—I've been trying to find you for the last five minutes. It's about the performing rights on the murder mystery. We've drawn a blank with the American publisher..."

In a moment, they were deep in conversation, Tor noting down details that Carol seemed to have filed away in her encyclopaedic memory. No sooner had she gone than Peter Butler, the press officer, approached with urgent questions about the photo calls next week, and a list of journalists who wanted to interview Lydia and Barrie. Tor, who apparently never used electronic devices, was making notes in his diary.

Marigold saw Don swing down from his perch and make for Tor, looking excited. "We've cracked it! The garden scene can be flown out, unhooked and stacked, and at the same time we fly in the gauze for the forest scene."

In a moment, Tor had switched his attention from press coverage to scene shifting. After congratulating Don, he gave Marigold a little push forward.

"Remember Marigold Aubrey? Our latest recruit." As Don shook hands with her, Marigold was rather shocked to see how young he was. The figure who had burst into Tor's office had been paint-bespattered and in shapeless overalls—and besides, she had been too nervous to really look at him. As he smiled at her, shaking his brown hair back from his face, Marigold felt gratitude to Tor that he had not passed on her silly comment of yesterday. She blushed again. No wonder Tor had been a little short with her.

"Are you enjoying rehearsals?" asked Don, shouting a little above the noise of all the stage crew, and she nodded, feeling suddenly that she was. He winked at her.

"Bet you can't wait until us lot have finished messing about here so you can start work properly."

"I've got an awful lot to learn first, don't worry!" Marigold laughed. Looking round for Tor, she saw that he had disappeared. "Oh, help, I'm lost now."

Don thought for a moment. "I'd say he's in wardrobe with Peggy and Tina. Do you know the way?"

Marigold made a wild guess, pointing in a random direction, and Don laughed.

"I'd better take you there." Casually grasping her arm, he steered her carefully through the morass of cables, woodwork, and people to yet another passage on the right hand side of the stage. In a few seconds, they were outside the door marked Wardrobe, and Don knocked confidently. As a voice answered, he opened the door and gently pushed her in.

"There you go. See you next week." Before Marigold could thank him, he was off again without a backward glance.

Inside the wardrobe room, it was comparatively peaceful. Costumes in all stages of completion hung from a long rail on one side of the room. On the other side was a generous full-length mirror.

Ironing boards and sewing machines were dotted about the room, and in one corner was an enormous table, on which Tor was sitting, swinging his legs and talking animatedly to a plump, grey-haired woman who had a pair of dressmaking scissors in her right hand. At a smaller table, a girl with a figure like a model and spiky blonde hair had stopped her sewing and was laughing at a joke Tor had just made.

Tor looked up and smiled as Marigold came in. "Ah, good—Don didn't kidnap you. Come and meet Peggy and Tina."

Marigold shook hands as Peggy's keen eye sized her up immediately.

"Ooh, aren't you tiny? Size eight, I should say. We could have done with you for the pantomime last Christmas—you remember, Tor? Those kids! They shot up about a foot each week—we were letting down and letting out every day, and Tina ran out of toffees to keep them happy."

Tor sprang up as a thought struck him. "While Marigold's here, why not arrange a time for a fitting next week? How are you getting on with Lydia?"

"Well, I won't say she's easy, but the frock fits, she can move in it, and of course she looks exquisite in it, so we're happy. Barrie's no problem, we've made for him before and he's really laid back about everything. And Brian's things can come out of stock."

Peggy pointed to a drawing that was tacked up on the noticeboard. "That's you, dear. Hope you like it."

Tina took the drawing down and handed it to Marigold. For once, Tor seemed in no hurry to move on, and no one was chasing him. He sat on the table with his arms folded and a smile on his face that reminded Marigold of a proud parent at a school prize-giving. Glancing up from the drawing, she could not help smiling back.

"Now you've met nearly the whole family," he said.

Marigold was touched by the pride and affection in his voice. He cared about all this, and these people clearly adored him.

She would have liked to thank him, except it would have sounded ridiculously schoolgirlish.

Marigold learned that the costumes for the play had been inspired by original eighteenth century paintings, but the costume designer, after consulting with Tor and Peggy, had cleverly adapted them to make them easier to move in. There were corsets, petticoats, and full skirts, but made of flexible materials to allow the actors to breathe and move. Polly's costume was a simple black and white maid's outfit with a dear little cap that Marigold knew would look perfect with her hair.

"And we've cut the pattern already from the measurements you sent us, so you'd better not have taken any inches off for vanity," said Peggy, eyeing her up again. "Next week we'll do a first fitting, then a final on Thursday, because you'll be needing the full costume for the press call and dress run on Friday—is that right, Tor?"

Marigold took a deep breath. "Suddenly, it all seems very close. The first night, I mean. And we've only had two days' rehearsal so far."

Tina nodded sympathetically. "Imagine how we feel—these sewing machines will be in overdrive, and we'll only know at the last minute if it's all as perfect as it should be."

"Ah, but it will be, Peggy. It always is," said Tor with absolute confidence.

Peggy gave him a fond smile. "We've never let you down yet, have we?"

A knock sounded at the door, and Jenny Warren put her head round. "Hello—is Tor here? There's a phone call for you in the office, and Carol says she is really sorry, it's something only you can deal with. It sounded like Lydia's agent."

Tor slid briskly off the table and gathered up his notebook and diary. "Jenny, could you be an angel and take care of Marigold? See you both tomorrow."

His only goodbye was a smile, and yet Marigold felt warmer toward him than she had all day. Why did he have to be so capricious?

As Jenny guided her back along the maze of passages to the auditorium, it was on the tip of Marigold's tongue to ask her how she managed to have a good working relationship with such an unpredictable, scary boss. But that wouldn't be kind—Jenny would be put on the spot. *She may even be living with him*, thought Marigold.

Jenny showed her the pass door, which led to the darkened auditorium, and wished her a friendly good night. Marigold wandered through the empty stalls, gazing up to the stage, where Don and his crew were still busy. Sinking into a plush seat, gazing up at the gilded plaster reliefs of cherubs and winged horses and the royal boxes with their maroon velvet swagged curtains, she felt a lurch of excitement as she visualized the curtain rising on the first night of *The Reluctant Rake,* and her first appearance as Polly.

A happy little shiver of anticipation swept over her, rather like the feeling she had as a child going on the Big Dipper. No going back now! Only ten more days' rehearsal!

"Oh, what am I doing? I've got to get home and go over my script again."

As she walked home, the sunshine of yesterday gave way to grey clouds massing in the east, and a chill wind suddenly made her shiver in her thin summer clothes.

CHAPTER FOUR

By the end of the first week, Marigold was beginning to know her way around the play, the theatre, and the delightful little town of Branchester. The slight awkwardness she had experienced with Barrie after the night in the pub soon evaporated, and they developed a friendly rapport. When he suggested meeting for a walk on Saturday afternoon, she had no problem with agreeing.

Luckily, Tor had been in a reasonably good mood for the rest of the week, and Marigold felt how, when he was bursting with positive energy, he was able to galvanize the cast into working long hours and finding that extra something in performance.

Marigold had been worried that after the row she had had with Tor over the pause, Lydia might think she was temperamental—but Lydia behaved as if the incident had never taken place. She did not exactly ignore Marigold, but she did not single her out for any special attention. And why should she?

Strangely, Helen Grant, who was playing the role of Lady Sophie's confidante, seemed to have fallen into that role offstage as well, for she and Lydia always sat together in the breaks, and once or twice they went out for meals together after rehearsals.

Marigold was particularly glad to see how Evelyn de Laurier was blossoming under Tor's considerate direction. She had learned her lines early on, and never got a move wrong, but Marigold wondered occasionally why Tor had cast her when she was, obviously, past her prime, and constantly needed confidence boosting.

Evelyn's acting did not have the spine-tingling quality of Lydia's or Barrie's work; the part of Lady Sophie's grandmother was a comically vicious old harridan, trying to marry her intelligent and spirited granddaughter off to all kinds of unsuitable men—mostly played by Brian Hancock in a variety of comic disguises—but there was one scene in the second act of the play where the old lady speaks bitterly about her own disappointments in love, and how she was herself forced to marry a man she did not love to escape from parents who would have crushed her spirit, and found only misery in the arms of a man who had no understanding of her at all.

It was a marvelous, poignant speech, a gift to a good actor, and every time Evelyn delivered it in rehearsals, Marigold was secretly willing her to give it that touch of theatre magic that would grip them, move them, and magnetize them—but sadly, so far it had not happened. No one ever said anything bad about Evelyn, and when she joined them for lunch they were always kind and considerate to her, but secretly Marigold wondered if Tor regretted casting her.

Marigold continued with her program of morning exercises, and was joined regularly by Robin and Helen. Robin was easy-going and optimistic, but he kept at a distance from the rest of the cast, partly because Branchester was his hometown. His social circle was huge, including school and family friends, and his partner, Toby, with whom he shared a flat.

Helen showed signs of wanting to get closer to Marigold, and had invited her to tea at her digs, but some instinct held her back from getting intimate with this older woman, whose mouth turned down at the corners and who so very frequently sat watching the others out of her rather small, sharp eyes.

Marigold had not set foot on the stage since her visit at the beginning of the week, but once or twice, she had seen Don Burlington in Carol Davies's office, and he had given her a friendly grin and a word of greeting.

She was now impatient to get into the proper theatre, having heard that the set construction was now finished and would be painted over the weekend, while the cast had their time off.

Peggy and Tina would also be working overtime at the weekend, and Marigold wondered how they kept so calm and cheerful with so little time off, for she knew that after a week of rehearsal, she really cherished her weekends.

Saturday morning dawned fine and sunny, a day for casual clothes—jeans and a tee shirt, with a loose cardigan in case the weather changed. Marigold was meeting Barrie in the market square at twelve; until then, she was free to wander about the shops in the old quarter of town, known as the Alleys, and perhaps to have lunch in a little café somewhere.

Her spirits were high as she skipped past the old clock tower in the center of the square, which was thronged with summer visitors. Sunshine streamed down on the whitewashed Sovereign Hotel, and cars were forced to proceed at a snail's pace along the road, crowded with pedestrians.

She headed to the Alleys, an area she loved already, with its narrow cobbled streets, crooked doors, and leaded windows. Most shops here dealt in antiques, smart clothes, souvenirs, and second-hand books—in the old days, this had been the center of Branchester's thriving fish industry. Most of the shops then sold wet fish or supplies to the fishing fleet, and the little cottages had been inhabited by fishermen and their families.

As she passed a downmarket antique shop with all kinds of junk piled untidily on the pavement outside, Marigold noticed that there was a live bird there, hunched up and miserable in a tiny Victorian birdcage.

"How could anyone be so cruel!"

She came closer, and the terrified little bird edged away from her.

"You're a linnet," said Marigold, and her hand went to her purse as she asked the shopkeeper how much he wanted for it.

"Oh, you have to buy it with the cage. It's real Victorian. I could let you have it for thirty-five."

"I don't want the cage, I want the bird set free," said Marigold.

"Sorry, love, the bird comes with the cage. Thirty-five."

Marigold opened her purse, but suddenly there was a hand gently grasping her wrist. Looking up, she saw Tor Douglas, and he did not look pleased.

"You won't sell the bird on its own?" he asked.

"What? Back off, mate. She's my customer; I'm not making her buy it."

Tor, with one swift movement, opened the door of the cage. The tiny bird immediately flew out of the cage and escaped to freedom, swooping joyously up to a nearby roof and bursting into song.

Marigold's eyes filled with joyful tears, but this magical moment was soon ended by the blustering shopkeeper, who rounded on Tor.

"What have you done? That was my property! You owe me thirty-five pounds!"

"I don't think so. That's a wild bird that should never have been in a cage, and if I see another one in this shop, I'll tell the RSPB and they'll send round a giant chicken to give you nightmares."

Marigold burst out laughing, but Tor was already gone, striding along the alley so fast she had to run to catch up with him. "Oh, please, Tor, wait—"

He stopped and turned, looking at her with an expression of surprise.

"I just wanted to say—that was fantastic. Thank you so much."

His face creased into a delightful grin.

On an impulse, she hugged him. He did not seem in the least embarrassed.

"I could do with a coffee," he said. "How about you?"

He did not take her hand, but as they walked along together, Marigold felt as comfortable with him as if she had known him for years.

They went into the coffee shop; he ordered an Americano and bought her a cappuccino with whipped cream on top.

"You would have spent your wages on that bird, wouldn't you?" he asked.

"Probably. I can't bear cruelty to animals. I had pets at home, and I used to get furious when my friends came round and teased them. I was too serious; you know how only children can be—too adult and civilized."

"Me too. Not civilized, I mean an only child. But I never had pets. I dreamed about owning a horse—but we were five floors up in a Glasgow tenement, so it had to stay a dream."

They finished their coffee and an awkward silence fell between them. Tor seemed in no hurry to leave, and Marigold did not want to tell him how she was spending the rest of the day.

"Have you any plans for the weekend?" he asked her—the very question she was dreading.

"I—well, I'm doing something this afternoon—meeting, er, a person," stumbled Marigold, red as a beetroot. "I don't really—"

"Later on? This evening?"

Marigold's mind raced as she wondered how long the walk with Barrie would take.

"I'm really, really sorry—" she was beginning, but his face had changed; his teasing smile was gone and he only said wearily, "It's Barrie Leicester, isn't it?"

"Yes, I'm going for a walk with him, not that it's any of your business. I'm not going out with him. We have a nice simple friendship, he just wants to show me around and make sure I'm not lonely. I'm not looking for a boyfriend."

Marigold was congratulating herself on standing up to Tor with this mature speech when, to her annoyance, she upset her coffee cup and couldn't stop the dregs dripping onto her jeans. She looked in her bag for a hankie, which she didn't have, and Tor silently gave her his napkin.

"Enjoy your weekend," he said suddenly, standing up. "See you Monday."

Before she could speak or protest, he was gone, threading his way easily through the crowded café.

Marigold scrubbed angrily at the coffee stain, which wouldn't come off. This was all Tor's fault! If it hadn't been for him cross-examining her, this would never have happened. Her sunny mood had clouded over, and Marigold arrived at the market square to meet Barrie with no sense of pleasurable anticipation.

He arrived a little late, wearing shades, and kissed her hand. "Madame is frowning. Have I kept her waiting?"

He was good-natured and considerate, and in a few minutes, he got her laughing and agreeing to have supper with him after the walk. "Jenny will be dropping by too, if that's okay?"

"Oh, yes, that's fine!" In fact, Marigold was delighted; that proved Barrie definitely did not have any designs on her, and he was such fun to be with, it wasn't surprising Jenny adored him.

Marigold had never enjoyed a grocery shopping expedition as much as that glorious Saturday spree with Barrie. He was like a little boy—wildly extravagant, loading the trolley with anything she pointed at. He insisted on real champagne, with a whole salmon and loads of cream to go with the fresh mangoes and pineapples. Endearingly honest, he admitted to a weakness for licorice allsorts.

When the trolley was full, he popped Marigold on top and whizzed along the aisles at the speed of light, making racing car noises as he screeched around corners. In quieter moments, they leaned over the freezer cabinet together, discussing purchases, and Marigold, undomesticated herself, was impressed by Barrie's enthusiasm for domestic life. Seemed like he really was the simple, would-be family man he had made himself out to be the other night.

When they reached the checkout, Barrie took off his sunglasses, setting off a babble of excited recognition first from the checkout girls, then from other female customers. Their getaway was delayed for a few moments as Barrie signed autographs and politely declined a request from the store manager to be photographed holding some of that week's special offers.

When their purchases were safely stowed in Barrie's vintage yellow MG, he opened the passenger door and ushered her in.

"Oh, what a glorious day to be getting away from it all!" Marigold said.

Barrie smiled at her excitement. "That's just what we're going to do. I'm going to make you fall in love with this part of the world."

Before long they were heading north along little winding lanes to a fishing village that Barrie said was an unspoiled gem. They spent all afternoon walking the cliffs, then scrambled down to a quiet beach—which Barrie said was always empty, even in the summer season—with a marsh that extended to the shore line, and the remains of an oak wood that the sea was gradually washing away. The white, scrubbed branches lifted stark fingers to the unrelentingly blue sky.

Barrie stroked a tree trunk, sadly shaking his head. "The first year I worked here, this wood was half a mile inland. All these dead trees were in full leaf."

They walked back inland, and the wood gradually came to life, with the green mossy limbs of the ash and oak trees creating shade. Barrie stopped and lit a cigarette under a horse chestnut tree.

"This one won't be here in another couple of years."

They went on to a bird reserve, and climbed a wooden ladder into a bird hide to watch the marsh birds wading and calling. Marigold was thrilled to see two herons flying ungracefully, their long legs waggling behind them. She asked Barrie for the names of the other birds, but he didn't know them, and Marigold found herself wondering if Tor ever visited this place—would he have known their names? She kept remembering the moment his strong and capable hands had freed the linnet, and her mind wandered from Barrie's humorous anecdotes about the world of television—even though, a week ago, she would have been hanging on his every word.

But as they headed back along the quiet roads with the lengthening evening shadows behind them, Barrie began to talk seriously about his life, and Marigold listened, enthralled, for this was now her world too, and she wanted to learn everything there was to know about it.

"Everyone always asks me about *Street Life*. To most people, that is Barrie Leicester, full stop. I'm not denying that it has been a massive part of my life for the last nine years and, in many ways, it's how I measure my development as an actor, and as a man. You know, I was only your age—what are you, twenty-one, twenty-two?—when I did the audition, and it was my first big telly break. I was in pieces the day Larry Miller called me in—the series producer. Lindy had walked out on me that morning—" He caught his breath, and his mouth twisted in a momentary grimace of pain. "And I was so terrified when I met him, so desperate not to put a foot wrong, that I hardly said a word. I did my piece and Larry said he'd call me later that day. By the evening, he hadn't rung. You can imagine how I was feeling."

Marigold nodded, remembering only too well her evening with Betsy—the pizzas, the stupid chatter, the desperate gaiety, and the fizzy wine.

"Well, finally, about eleven, he rang me. He was charming—but I hadn't got the part."

"You *didn't* get it? But—you—"

Barrie slowed down, driving with more care and thought. "One of those cruel strokes of fate gave me my break while robbing someone else of theirs. Ever heard of an actor called Courtney White?"

"No. Don't think so."

"Well, he was the one who they originally wanted for Eddie. They were right too—he would have been brilliant. And he really was a biker, like the character. He had an accident on his bike the day after I auditioned, and it was such a mess—he had to have his leg amputated. Larry phoned me straight away to ask if I was still interested. And that was it. I became Eddie."

Barrie looked infinitely sad as he lit another cigarette. Was it her imagination, or were there real tears in his eyes?

"That taught me two things. First—no matter how good you are, if you get the breaks, its 99 percent luck. And second—no one's indispensable. If it hadn't been me, someone else would have done it just as well."

"I so don't agree, and nor do thousands of people who love you because you created Eddie. Everyone knows he's the best thing in *Street Life*. All my friends were in love with you. Your picture was on a thousand bedroom walls."

Barrie laughed, and pressed harder on the accelerator. The car roared along the deserted road.

"After the first series, I felt like a kid in a sweetshop. Producers wanted me, agents were killing each other to get me—someone even wanted me to record songs! If you've ever heard me sing, you'll know what a joke that would have been. Then the theatre work started coming, and nine years later, the dream goes on..."

He fell silent, and seemed to be almost in a trance. Not a very happy one, for the expression on his face was that of a lost and wistful child.

*

Barrie's flat overlooked the old seafront and esplanade, on the top floor of a huge old Edwardian house, which had been converted and modernised. Marigold, staggering under several of their shopping bags, was grateful for the lift that whizzed them up to the penthouse.

Once inside, Marigold could only stand and stare. Luxury and opulence beckoned. The soft pile of the carpet invited her to kick off her shoes and a large squashy sofa opened its arms to her. Barrie flicked a remote, and gentle guitar music filled the flat. She found a glass of chilled white wine in her hand, as he disappeared into the kitchen to start the meal, refusing her tentative offer of help.

She stretched out luxuriously on the sofa, suddenly aware of her tiredness after a day in the open air. It was such bliss to know that there would be no work tomorrow, no rehearsal room, and no Tor, with his brooding brow and smouldering eyes.

She took a gulp of the wine, which was very dry indeed, wishing Barrie had added some mineral water, but too comfortable to get up and fetch herself some. She was willing to bet that the kitchen was brilliantly well equipped and well stocked. Glancing around the room, she noticed fresh flowers in graceful vases, and none of the usual clutter she would have expected to find in a bachelor flat. Maybe he had a cleaner. The windows offered her endless vistas of blue sea under a darkening summer sky, and the music lulled her charmingly to sleep as she put down her wine, closed her eyes, and lay back...

Ages later, she was woken by something tickling her nose, and Barrie, wearing an apron and standing over her with a feather duster, was wagging a reproachful finger at her.

"This is the first time I've ever bored a beautiful woman to sleep," he sighed, as Marigold struggled into a sitting position.

"I am so sorry—how awful of me! Is there anything I can do? I think the sea hypnotized me a bit..." She saw how dark it was outside, with only the faintest streaks of light in the sky. "How long have I been asleep?"

"Oh, it's after nine, but don't look so distraught. Dinner's ready."

They went into the kitchen, a long room with skylights and a circular white table. It managed to be both spacious and compact, with a bank of dials and switches for all the ovens, hobs, and microwaves.

The table was lit with red candles, but it was only laid for two. By one place, there was a single long-stemmed red rose.

"Er—didn't you say Jenny was going to come for dinner?"

Barrie was frowning slightly as he opened the wine. "Oh, she sent me a text—she's held up at some meeting at the theatre, poor love; they work her too hard." He took her glass and filled it. "Now, Madame is served."

At first, Marigold thought the dinner might be slightly awkward, but Barrie was more charming than ever—witty, funny, generous, and occasionally, a very good listener. He had every right to be proud of his cooking too, for the perfectly poached salmon was followed by a delicious salad, followed by a pudding that combined grapes, meringues, fresh cream, and ginger—a dish that Barrie said he had invented.

"I have such a weakness for puddings," he confessed, having a third helping, "so I make do with one a week. It would never do for Eddie to wobble as he leaps astride his bike."

"Will there be another series?" asked Marigold, wondering whether Barrie had any say in the choice of other actors in the series. Might there be a part for her or Betsy?

"Oh, I think there's one more, starting in September—that's what they always say, just one more. I know it won't last forever—just as long as people like Eddie. That's why I make sure never to forget my audience."

"I wonder what I'll be doing in September?" mused Marigold.

He answered her challengingly, holding her gaze across the table. "What would you like to be doing?"

"Shakespeare, or something classical, in London. Isn't that what we all want?"

"Do we?"

"It probably doesn't mean anything to you—I expect you've already achieved all your professional ambitions. But I'm only starting, and I want so much—and there seems an impossibly long way to go."

"And what would you be prepared to do to succeed?" Barrie's voice had taken on an edge she couldn't quite identify.

"Oh, almost anything. I'd work seven days a week for nothing. I really want to get somewhere." Marigold faltered as he stared at her fiercely and uncompromisingly, as if he was setting her some kind of test.

"Anything at all?"

"Oh, well, anything legal. And of course I would never compromise my integrity."

His lips twitched. "And what, in your opinion, would endanger your lovely young integrity?"

"You know what I'm talking about. I'm not getting into bed with anyone to get a job, no matter how good it might be."

Barrie's face suddenly relaxed, and he smiled at her so dazzlingly that she felt her head spin—or was it the effect of the wine?

"I am so glad you said that, Goldie. Hold on to it. I've seen so many broken dreams, met so many fallen angels. Don't become one of them. The dream you catch might just be a cheap and tarnished thing, not real gold, only flaking plaster and faded gilt."

"You sound so bitter, Barrie, you're scaring me!"

He turned away. "I'm sorry. Don't be scared. Just remember that everyone has their price. Maybe I had mine."

His face had that hunted, lost expression that it had worn the first night in the pub, and it made Marigold want to put her arms round him in a motherly way. He was such a fascinating mixture; she never knew what would happen next when he was around.

What happened next was that Barrie carried their coffees into the sitting room, dropped the blinds using another remote, and made more music surge into the room. It was a slow and somber orchestral piece that was unfamiliar to her, and whether it was the effect of the music or the wine she could not say, but she began to feel unwelcome physical stirrings of excitement as she sat on the sofa next to where he was carelessly sprawled.

Slowly, he wriggled out of his jacket, then the tie he had put on for dinner. He ran his hand through his curls and undid the top button of his shirt. He sighed with pleasure, not even seeming to notice that she was sitting next to him, clutching her drink, uneasy and wide awake.

Suddenly he extended a foot toward her. "Be an angel and take my shoe off."

Marigold undid the lace and slid the shoe onto the floor, where it fell soundlessly onto the deep pile of the carpet. He offered her his other foot, and without a word, she took off the other shoe. There was something so nakedly intimate about these wordless actions that Marigold's heart began to thump; this had to be the overture to something that Barrie had planned for her, had intended from the first moment they had met that morning.

Yet, as she looked at him, he seemed far from consumed with passion; he half-lay against the soft cushions with his long, fair lashes against his cheek. In repose, his face looked younger, undefended, the fine line of his jaw curving up to the half-concealed, rather neatly tucked in ears and his perfectly symmetrical hairline, the broad forehead and those tumbled, caressable curls.

With his eyes closed, Barrie began gently humming along to the music and Marigold tried to relax and lie back on the sofa, which was too soft and persuasive; it suggested she too should yield and grow soft.

She made no move, listening to the music in silence. Maybe it wasn't too late for Jenny to arrive. She stopped her breath as Barrie sat up and leaned over to her, his eyes very wide.

"Do you mind if I do—this?" He reached out, and before she had time to object, he had gently pulled the ribbon from her hair, letting it fall loosely about her shoulders. With a sigh, he pulled her closer to him, interlacing his hands in her hair, and then his mouth was pressed hard on hers, and he was pulling her to lie full-length beside him.

Marigold wrenched herself free, appalled and angry—angry with herself that she had not suspected all along that this was going to happen.

His eyes snapped open, and he was gazing at her now in a way that meant deep trouble. How could she have been so stupid! And why was it so hard to go along with what he wanted—why was she so suddenly repelled by his kiss and his mooning face, a face like a sheep's? She didn't want to kiss him or have him touching her. She couldn't go through the motions of lovemaking. She wasn't available to any man—hadn't she made it clear to him? Her heart was pounding now, pounding along with the music, which was reaching a slow but certain crescendo. He was stroking her hair; he was so certain of himself, that he would get what he wanted.

"Don't be frightened," he was saying caressingly. "You're very young, aren't you? I'll take care of you, I promise."

As if in answer to her prayer, his phone started to ring. With a savage gesture, he flung himself off the sofa and snatched it up. Even in his disheveled and overexcited state, he managed to inject a note of sympathy and kindness into his voice as he answered.

"Darling! What a pity, I'm so sorry. No, I'll be fine. See you tomorrow. Don't beat yourself up over it, promise me? Good girl. Okay. Bye."

He put the phone down.

"That was Jenny. You see, I *did* invite her. This evening wasn't part of some carefully staged seduction. You just don't know how attractive your innocence is. Do you?"

He came close to her again and reached out for her, but she pulled away, clearing her throat nervously.

"Barrie, I don't know what to say. I don't—I didn't think—I like you, of course, but this is all too—"

His face darkened. "You seemed very happy a few minutes ago."

"It was such a surprise. I was in shock."

He sat on the arm of the sofa, watching.

Marigold felt like a mouse under the eye of a horribly skilled and patient cat.

"Barrie. I need to say this. I definitely don't—not now, I mean, not tonight, and I'm not sure if ever—you are very attractive but—oh, God, this is so difficult—I'm desperately sorry if I misled you or hurt your feelings, but I can't, I just can't."

She knew she was making a complete fool of herself. Struggling for words, stammering and blushing, she was behaving like an idiot, while he, experienced and famous and popular—he was sitting on the arm of the sofa, watching and waiting.

"Okay, I hear you," he said finally. "But you know something? You're so beautiful that I can't help wanting to kiss you, even while you're saying 'no' with that wonderful mouth."

He reached his hand out to her, resting it on her shoulder. "I can't pretend I don't want you, because you know I do, and I usually get what I want. You talk about feelings—well, feelings can be very confusing. I don't, right at this moment, know exactly what my feelings are about you. Why don't we explore those feelings, just a little? Maybe going to bed will help us understand things more clearly."

He leaned toward her, and fearing that everything was getting more and more out of control, Marigold sprang up and took a few steps away from him.

"No. Barrie, I mean it. No."

Suddenly, to her horror, he was on his knees in front of her, gripping her thighs, pressing his face into her belly and shaking with sobs. He lifted his face to her and she saw that he was crying real tears that were trickling down his cheeks as he caught his breath and bit his lip.

"Oh, Barrie, don't, please—"

"I want you. I want to hold you oh so gently, in my arms all night and never let you go. I want you to hold me, I want you to do whatever you want with me, touch me, kiss me, just be mine for this one night. Please say you will. Darling, darling Marigold, please."

This was agonizing. She felt pulled in two. She didn't want to go to bed with him—but had she led him on in some way? And was she responsible for the pain he seemed to be suffering now?

But the more he begged her, the less she wanted to stay. She had to get away.

"I can't. Don't do this to me, Barrie. Please—let me go home."

Slowly, he let go of her and got to his feet. He took a packet of cigarettes from a low table and lit one, not stopping to offer one to her. Their eyes met, but what a different face she was seeing now. His mouth was set in the stubborn pout of a thwarted child.

"I can't force you, obviously," he said coldly. "You'd better go."

Feeling utterly in disgrace, Marigold collected her belongings and stood by the door of the flat, waiting to be dismissed.

"Goodbye, then," she whispered, while he leaned against the window, looking out, smoking, distant.

"You're just a frightened little virgin, in spite of those 'come to bed' eyes," was all he said, still with his back to her.

Marigold didn't know how she managed to get home, but when at last she was safely in her single bed at Mrs. Harbour's, tears of humiliation overwhelmed her, and she cried herself to sleep.

CHAPTER FIVE

As Marigold arrived at the theatre early on Monday morning, a grey hand of misery squeezed her heart.

She had spent Sunday very quietly and alone, hardly venturing out in case she should meet anyone from the theatre. She knew that if she ran into Barrie again, she would simply burst into tears.

A cosy and calorific Sunday tea with Mrs. Harbour in a reminiscent mood had first soothed her, then made her desperately homesick; she fled to her room and wrote a string of emails to her parents, Betsy, and even a few old school friends, but said nothing to anyone about what had happened—or not happened—in Barrie's flat. Then she ran a bath, and went to bed at about nine o'clock, only to lie awake until long after midnight, going over and over the events of Saturday. Had she led him on? At what moment had he decided she was going to bed with him? Did she owe him anything for all his generosity—he'd given up the whole day to entertain her.

And how on earth was she going to be able to stand on stage kissing him, with all the cast watching? How would she be able to stop thinking about the dreadful scene in his flat? Wouldn't he be thinking the same?

By chance, the first person she met when she arrived at the theatre that morning was Don Burlington. He loped along behind her, catching her up easily, and slowed his pace to walk with her. Her heart sank as she realized he was going to stay with her all the way to the stage—she wouldn't have a chance to compose herself.

"Well, it's all ready." He smiled. "Hope you like it."

She forced a smile. "Does that mean your work is nearly over?"

He chuckled, and she saw that he was carrying a hammer and some nails.

"Oh dear no. I was in at eight o'clock for a tour of inspection by Mr. Marchmont, and he's already had three tiny tantrums. We'll be running round like headless chickens until he's happy."

He pushed open the door for her, and she soon found herself backstage. Even in her mood of misery she at once noticed the pungent combination of smells—wood, size, hot lights, and fresh paint—that for her was the essence of theatre. Gratefully, she breathed it in. She hoped Don would leave her alone to prepare quietly for her coming ordeal, but he was in a sociable mood and beckoned her over to the center of the stage, gesturing all around him.

"Well—what do you think? Quite a transformation, isn't it?"

Marigold could only gasp. Don was not exaggerating. The room she was standing in quite simply *was* Lady Sophie's drawing room.

The walls were painted, but so cleverly that they looked real, with eighteenth century striped wallpaper, grey and green sprigged with pink, and hung with painted-on portraits. Upstage were the two enormous windows with velvet curtains, embellished with cherubs and flowers. Over the huge mantelpiece hung a vast mirror with an ornate gilt frame, the mirror glass sprayed lightly with grey paint so it would not reflect the stage lights back to the audience.

The floor was carpeted and crowded with furniture laid out exactly as Jenny had taped it in the rehearsal room but now solidly three-dimensional and upholstered in cream chintz with a pale grey Regency stripe: a chaise longue, two beautiful armchairs, several small tables, and a dear little piano, which Marigold, in her role as Polly the maid, would frequently find herself dusting.

Here too was Lady Sophie's writing desk, where Polly was to discover Lord Harcourt's love letter. As the scene came vividly to her, a cold chill struck at Marigold's heart and her excitement evaporated.

"You've done an amazing job," she said to Don, but even as she tried to inject some enthusiasm into her voice, she knew that it sounded wooden and lifeless.

"Are you okay? You look really pale—" Just then a furious voice started squeaking from the wings, and Don froze, a comic expression of impending doom on his face.

"Where IS that man? DON!" the cry sounded again, and Don shrugged.

"Dear Noel. He's having a whole litter of kittens," Don said. "I'll have to go."

Marigold walked around the set and made herself familiar with all the exits and entrances. Her props had already been laid out neatly on a table in the wings on the left, or prompt, side of the stage, lit with fluorescent working lights. The curtain, of course, was raised.

As Marigold stood on the stage looking out into the empty auditorium, she cheered herself up by imagining an audience on its feet, applauding madly. She swept a deep curtsey to the empty seats.

She was sure she had been alone, but suddenly there was the sound of clapping and laughter, and the next minute, Lydia Dawlish came sweeping down the aisle.

"Bravo, Polly," she called, and Marigold was relieved to hear that her voice was not unkind. "This time next week, my dear..."

*

Just before ten o'clock, the stage was clear of workmen and the theatre had fallen quiet as Marigold sat in the stalls, scanning the pages of a script she already knew by heart. She did not want Barrie to catch her unawares, so she kept her head in her script, shrinking down in her seat so she would remain as invisible as possible.

The cast began arriving: Tor, very occupied with Jenny and a page of notes, Brian and Robin, chatting about skiing, Helen, late and out of breath and, finally, Barrie.

He stepped onto the stage as if it were his kingdom, shoulders thrown back and his hands stuck in the pockets of his black trousers. She noticed straight away that he was wearing Eddie's trademark black leather jacket, and that his hair, freshly washed, glittered gold and silver under the lights.

He looked out to the auditorium, for a moment seeming to stare directly at Marigold. Without acknowledging her, he made a slow, dramatic turn and studied the entire set, nodding. Finally, he turned back to the auditorium and, shielding his eyes from the lights, looked for Tor.

"Lovely, lovely," he breathed, gesturing at the set.

Tor returned his wave and continued talking to Jenny. Five minutes passed, and he looked up from his notebook. It was exactly ten o'clock. "Right, everybody onstage," he said briskly, and Marigold put down her script and climbed the stairs to the stage. There was, it felt to her, an acre of soft red Turkey carpet between herself and Barrie, and that was how she wanted to keep it, for as long as she possibly could. She tried not to think about the flirting and kissing they would soon be forced to do, while pretending enjoyment.

"Can you all stand in line for a moment—Lydia center, Barrie, Marigold—come along, Marigold—Helen, other side of Lydia, Brian. Robin, you could stand either end, you choose. Fine. Now—out front please, and smile—lovely. That's how you'll be standing a week from today. As if we all need reminding. So to work, my darlings, and can I have the stage clear of everyone except Act One beginners."

Marigold and Lydia were the Act One beginners, onstage as the curtain rose, so they took up their positions—Lydia languishing with her embroidery and the chaise longue while Marigold found her first prop—a silver tray on which she would deliver calling cards and letters to her mistress—already set for her on a small table under the window. She marveled at the efficiency of Jenny Warren, who must have been doing this on Saturday, when she was working so late.

"And—off you go, and can we have a timing on Act One, please Jenny?" called Tor, and Marigold felt her concentration coming back as she became Polly, waiting on Lady Sophie, who threw down her embroidery and asked Polly to bring her a cup of chocolate.

After the first scene, Polly left the stage while Lady Sophie wittily and conclusively refused to marry the elderly Judge, her first suitor. It was impossible to avoid Barrie for much longer, for it would be Polly's job to show him in, and as she came offstage, Marigold nearly collided with him.

Offstage, it was totally dark and she couldn't see the expression on his face. He did not speak to her—but that might have been because Tor had already given them a lecture about good manners backstage, and having respect for your fellow actors by not whispering or chatting in the wings while others were performing. So both of them stood silently waiting for Polly's cue, and she had to bounce on stage to announce, "Lord Harcourt is come to visit, madam."

As soon as Barrie made his entrance as the debonair lord, swirling an old rehearsal cloak about him, he handed Polly his gloves, cloak, and hat, giving her a saucy wink, just as they had rehearsed.

Marigold was so relieved that she could then exit the stage; then she looked around for a place to put Lord Harcourt's discarded clothes. In a few moments she would be called back to escort him out, and it did not seem worth walking all the way over to the props table, so she was pleased to find a useful nail on the back of a nearby piece of scenery and hung the cloak from that, tucking the hat and gloves above it.

Before she made another entrance, though, Tor had stopped the rehearsal and made Barrie and Lydia run the scene again, then again, as he said it "wasn't sparkling enough."

After that came the moment, Marigold had been dreading. Tor said, "Can you pick it up now from scene four—Polly, Lord Harcourt, and, stand by, the butler."

Marigold, feeling physically ill, went and stood onstage. In a very few moments, after some light-hearted banter, she and Barrie would be kissing. Under her breath, she muttered to herself, "It's not Barrie, it's Lord Harcourt."

The scene went well at first and Marigold, studying Barrie closely, marveled at his professional detachment. He really seemed to be playing the scene with just as much easy enjoyment as he had shown last week, and when he caught her eye, his only expression was one of amused interest.

Finally, the moment arrived that she had been dreading: Lord Harcourt steals an unexpected kiss. In spite of herself, she flinched as she felt his lips press briefly on hers. The script demanded that she pushed him away indignantly, and that he begged her pardon, but then they had to kiss again, much more passionately.

The second kiss was an absolute disaster. Marigold could tell that Barrie was finding the kiss as difficult as she was. She closed her eyes and tried desperately to lose herself in the character of Polly, but all she could see in her mind was the penthouse flat, the carpet, hearing the insistent music, and Barrie, pulling her along the sofa to lie next to her…

And how could he help thinking exactly the same things?

As they drew apart and looked uncertainly at each other, Tor's voice boomed through the stalls. "What on earth is going on here?"

He bounded along the stalls and leapt up on the stage, staring at them both searchingly. "That was appalling. You both look as if you were going to be sick."

Barrie glanced briefly at Marigold, then cast his eyes down to the floor like a little boy in trouble with his teacher. Marigold, on the other hand, could not take her eyes away from Tor's strong mouth and blazing eyes.

"Last week, you had it. This scene was almost perfect—lots of crackle and buzz. Now you're like a pair of wooden puppets."

Tor's comments were mostly aimed at Barrie, which was a great relief to Marigold.

"What are you playing at, Barrie? Go back to the first kiss."

Barrie gave him a pleading look, which Tor ignored.

"I don't care if she's got a cold, I don't care if you hate her perfume, I don't care if she makes you want to throw up—the script says kiss her. So kiss her."

Marigold closed her eyes and waited. It couldn't get much more painful than this.

Barrie's second attempt drew an explosion of fury from Tor.

"Barrie! Worse and worse! Have you never kissed a woman? Flirted with a woman? Tease her, drive her mad."

Marigold wished the stage would open up and swallow her. She could see the rest of the cast watching eagerly, enjoying the unexpected comedy. An awful certainty came to her that they were guessing what had happened between her and Barrie at the weekend.

Tor's face was relentless, his determination palpable, and she knew he would not let them leave that scene until he was happy with everything in it, including the dreaded kisses.

Every time Barrie's lips met hers, she felt his mouth stiffen rebelliously and his body pull away as if she had the plague. It was too vivid in her mind's eye—those awful moments when he had clung to her, abasing himself, begging her to go to bed with him, hot tears rolling down his cheeks, and then his icy parting comment. No wonder he was finding the kiss difficult. The only thing that made this moment bearable was that Tor was not attacking her with the same vigor he was using to tear strips off Barrie.

"That's technically all right," he grudgingly conceded after their fifth attempt, "but there's not an ounce of passion here."

"I think I might have a touch of flu," Barrie was beginning to say weakly, when Tor interrupted him.

"Don't make excuses. The scene is unrecognizable. We'll look at it again tomorrow." Before either of them could protest, he vaulted off the stage and went back to his seat in the stalls.

Marigold hardly remembered the rest of that day. She was aware of walking through Polly's scenes, saying the lines, remembering the correct moves, and making exits and entrances as if hypnotized. She even managed to squeeze out a few tears in the letter scene, but it was as if her real self was wrapped in layers of cotton wool.

By lunchtime, she was ready to drop. Although Tor had not singled her out, she was on edge, constantly expecting him to make an example of her as he had with Barrie, who seemed able to take any amount of humiliation. She felt too wretched to eat anything, and stayed in the theatre while everyone else went to buy baguettes. Barrie was laughing as he went out, his arm around Helen Grant, drinking in the sympathy of the others for his baptism of fire from Tor.

At the end of the day, Marigold, feeling about six inches tall, was putting her script away and preparing to leave.

"Not so fast, Polly," Tor's voice sang out in the darkened auditorium, and a moment later he was beside her. He seemed to be as full of energy as he had been at ten that morning. "Cancel your plans for this evening. You're coming with me."

Marigold stared at him incredulously. "I know I didn't do very well today, but I—"

"Please," he said suddenly, and her eyes were, as always, transfixed by his mesmeric gaze. "Please give me an hour. It's more work, I know, it's all I'm asking, only work, but you'll see and feel the difference tomorrow. I promise you, you will be a lot happier tomorrow."

Dumbly, she nodded. She followed him out of the theatre and stood as he hailed a taxi with a swift, confident gesture.

"The Sovereign, if you would be so kind," he said, and the next minute they were bowling through the streets of Branchester. Marigold lay back against the luxurious upholstery, wondering if the snooty doorman at the swankiest hotel in town would allow her in wearing jeans and a tee shirt, and whether she could get through the next hour without bursting into tears.

As they walked up the steps, Marigold realized that her fantasy of being refused entry was miles away from the reality; the doorman touched his hat to Tor, disheveled and in his working clothes, the receptionist smiled and welcomed Marigold warmly, and as they entered the dining room the manager hurried forward, greeting Tor by name, and showed him to the window table of the sumptuous dining room.

"I'm having the duck," he announced abruptly, "and if you've any sense, so will you. Everything else tastes like stewed flannel."

She noticed how the occasional word betrayed his Scottish origins—was that so in rehearsals? Or maybe only when he was off duty, relaxing, as he seemed to be tonight. He was waving aside the wine list, ordering mineral water for both of them, making humorous small talk with the waiter, and suddenly turning his unsettling attention on her.

"You're troubled about something, aren't you?" he said. "You give yourself away. Your eyes change color—when you are worried, they turn quite green. All the blue drains away, and you look like a drowned kitten."

Marigold giggled, then wondered if he would be offended, and tried to look mature and slightly worried.

"So—what's the problem? Barrie won't leave you alone? Or are you madly in love with him and he's giving you the cold shoulder?

He has other habits, I know, but those are two of his less endearing traits—"

"Tor," began Marigold, trying to stop her voice trembling. "Whatever you may think has happened between Barrie and myself, it really isn't anything to do with you."

Tor folded his arms and shook his head. "Wrong. As soon as it affects your work, it's my business. And wouldn't you agree with me that your work today really wasn't up to the standard you set yourself last week?"

His tone was so reasonable, and his face wore such an expression of concern that Marigold felt herself suddenly relax. She could trust this man; his interest was purely professional.

"I'm sorry I disappointed you today," she said, looking directly into his eyes as if she was not in the least scared of him.

Gently, he clasped one of her hands between his, and squeezed it. "Not me. You let yourself down."

"Tor, is it okay if I tell you something in confidence? I spent Saturday with Barrie. I really like—thought I really liked him, and I thought he was just a friend, you know, nothing more, because really I hardly knew him, and he doesn't know me at all—so we went for a walk, and he was so kind and showed me beaches and stuff and we had fun, just laughing and enjoying ourselves and—oh, this sounds so stupid now—after we spent the day together I went back to his flat and he cooked me a meal. And—oh, this makes me sound more and more like an idiot—it just hadn't occurred to me that he was expecting, or hoping, or had plans for—and I had to just escape, get out, and he was furious—oh, it was awful..." Marigold couldn't stop tears from starting to her eyes, and even though she blotted them fiercely with her napkin, here she was, crying in front of Tor, crying like a baby.

He waited until she had recovered herself, then leaned forward and whispered, "You were brave."

She managed a shaky smile. It seemed incredible to think that she had almost hated him in rehearsal today.

"So that was the problem. Every time we had to do that kiss—well, he knew what I was thinking, and I knew what he was thinking, and we just messed it up every time—and now I don't know if we can ever get it right."

Tor sat silent for a while, looking down at his plate. She wondered if he thought she was completely stupid and childish.

He caught her anxious look, and a curious and hard-to-interpret expression flitted across his face.

Was he trying to find a nice way of saying she was no good?

"You know, you are playing in the big league with this cast," he finally said, "and whatever you may be feeling just at the moment, there are no cracks showing. You've just learned a hard lesson, and it's probably made you feel about two inches tall, but later on, you might be grateful. I'd say you are a warm-hearted, impulsive person, and Barrie Leicester is a charming, likeable, enchanting man. However, he is entirely self-obsessed. He'll never do anything unless there is a payoff. He also nurtures an enormous ego, and you have bruised it badly. So you're on his cold shoulder list for the next few days. Fortunately, I can tell you he is finding it just as hard to do his job as you are, so I would guess he'll stop punishing you very soon. Please don't think I'm a killjoy—you're entitled to some fun on your day off, but I'm also disillusioned with actors like Barrie who always get what they want, and to hell with other people."

She was hanging on his words, but, as always, he left her wanting more. Their food arrived and he attacked it with a hearty appetite. There was nothing she could do but follow suit. He had dismissed the incident from his mind, and she felt a wave of gratitude for the trouble he was taking.

She didn't want him to think she was self-obsessed too, like Barrie, or unaware of all the other problems that Tor was solving every day, so, after they had finished their meal and had some coffee, she plucked up her courage to ask a question.

"I love the set. Will we get a chance to meet Noel Marchmont?"

"Highly unlikely. Why would you want to, anyway? Dreadful man." Tor crumpled his napkin vigorously as he spoke.

"But he's famous! And he has done a brilliant job."

"My dear," said Tor. "Learn one of the first lessons of theatre. Credit rarely goes where it is truly due. Noel makes a song and dance and gets mega publicity. Don builds the set and makes it work and hides in his workshop when the journalists come round and never gets a mention."

"But Don's only the carpenter!" Marigold burst out. "Surely the design, the inspiration, came from Noel's original drawings?"

"Those scribbles? Let me show them to you sometime."

"Well, if he's so useless and difficult, why do you use him?"

Tor glared at her and she wondered, yet again, if she had gone too far. But then he gave a snort of laughter. "Politics—like everything else in this business. Everything in life is ruled by compromise."

With an expansive gesture, he brought the waiter scurrying to their table.

"Would you ask Leon to book Miss Aubrey a taxi for ten thirty?" he asked. "We'll be in Room 344."

"Yes, of course, Mr. Douglas," murmured the waiter, sliding Marigold an ambiguous sideways glance.

Was she one of a series of women that Tor had entertained in room 344? She hadn't realized till now that he was staying here. No wonder they all treated him like a favorite nephew.

"That should give us plenty of time, don't you think?"

Tor said this calmly enough, but it made her heart lurch suddenly. What did he have in mind? Was she expected to agree to whatever was asked of her?

Her head was whirling—she was scarcely able to take in Tor's amusing commentary on the hotel's architectural peculiarities as he steered her into the brass-embellished Edwardian lift, in which they made a wheezing ascent to the third floor.

Following him along the corridor to his room, Marigold was shaking. He really could do whatever he wanted with her—he was the boss.

Tor's room was disgracefully untidy; in one corner was a large desk covered with paperwork—half-opened box files, scripts, two in-trays of papers and letters and a spike impaling bills and receipts.

The large window was wide open and the breeze created further havoc, blowing papers onto the bed. It was a king-sized bed that dominated the whole room. Unmade, and with black satin sheets and pillowcases that, to Marigold's alarmed gaze, spelled seduction. A pair of crumpled red pajamas was flung across one of the pillows.

Tor seemed not to notice the chaos, and sat in a large armchair on one side of the fireplace, gesturing at Marigold to sit in its companion on the other side. Before she could, she had to move an untidy heap of Tor's clothes—a confused mixture of clean socks, shirts, and vests. She stood awkwardly in the middle of the room wondering where to put it all and if Tor ever opened his wardrobe.

"Good, you're getting into character," he said, seemingly amused. "Or is Polly taking over your life?"

"I can't sit down, that's all," she said. "Where shall I put them?"

"Oh, anywhere—on the bed, why not?" he answered carelessly.

She put the clothes on top of the pajama trousers, which she was finding horribly distracting, and then sat down.

"Get yourself comfortable, don't perch on the edge like that," commanded Tor.

"I'm perching because I have no idea what's going to happen. If I look nervous, it's because I didn't expect the evening to be ending in your bedroom," she said, as cheekily as she dared.

Tor threw his head back and laughed. "Oh, Miss Mouse, you are a delight. I said work, didn't I? Or have you forgotten?"

"I don't know." Marigold was beginning to feel a blush creeping over her face. "You didn't really make it clear, and I'm just your employee—I can't be questioning you and disagreeing with you, even out of work hours, can I?"

Tor stopped laughing. He rose from his chair and, crossing to Marigold, he knelt down on the carpet in front of her. Even kneeling down, he was still taller than she was. His voice was gentle. "Unlike some directors, I never take advantage of my position to intimidate women into bed with me," he said, looking at her as an equal, a look she felt able to return.

"It's a confusing world we inhabit, I know," he continued, "and the reason why lots of us, talented young actors and directors, lose their way and go under is because they are unable to distinguish between truth and illusion. Feelings are teased and stretched onstage beyond endurance, and it sometimes becomes impossible to know whether you feel, or only act a feeling. Are you with me?"

Marigold nodded. He knew exactly where she was, right now.

"Good. So, let's do some serious work." He stood up and held out a hand to her, and she sprang to her feet, feeling energized. He handed her a script.

"Oh, but I know this," she protested. "I know every word—"

"I know you do. But what we are about to do is an old drama school exercise that I haven't had time to do with you in rehearsal, and for that, we need a text. It's a pleasure, let me tell you, to be working with someone who has been so well trained, and whose training is still so fresh."

Marigold always felt, when he paid her a compliment, that there would be a double edge to it, and sure enough, the other side was not long in coming.

"I feel sometimes, though, that you are just a little bit too— too careful with Polly. You have her moves, and her lines, and her voice just right, but you never relax and just have fun with her. I haven't yet felt you being inhabited by Polly."

Marigold bit her lip. It was a favorite criticism of her teachers at drama school. Were her bad mannerisms so glaringly obvious?

"Now, I know that today has been extremely difficult for you, and that most of your time onstage was being spent trying not to think about the love scenes with Lord Harcourt. But, up till now, you haven't given us enough. The audience has got to enjoy Polly, they have to understand what it must be like to be a girl from a poor family suddenly rescued from starvation and given the privilege of waiting on a great lady. Can you tell me what Polly might do on her day off, if she has one?"

Marigold had already played this game alone, in order to make her sense of Polly more three-dimensional, and she entered into the game with enjoyment.

As they continued, with Tor explaining everything so knowledgeably and vividly, answering her questions about the social customs and habits, showing his insights into the lives of Polly and her household, Marigold began to have an idea of just how much work he had put into this play, long before the first rehearsal had begun. He was patient, good-humoured, and witty, but always kind.

After an hour of intricate work on the text, going through Polly's major speeches with a fine-tooth comb and in a variety of styles, Marigold felt her concentration slipping away. Her eyes were beginning to close. Tor put the script down.

"Let's take a break. Would some coffee be a good idea?"

"A very good idea," said Marigold, trying not to yawn as she thought longingly of her single bed at Mrs. Harbour's.

Tor scrabbled about on his desk until he found the phone and rang for coffee, checking on Marigold's taxi at the same time. Marigold felt such relief that there was no uncertainty about how this evening was going to end.

"I'm sorry I can't let you go just yet, because we haven't looked at your most important scenes—"

Marigold's heart dropped to the floor. The Lord Harcourt love scenes. The ones she had been hoping he'd forgotten.

Timidly, she offered, "I really don't have a problem with those, really I don't, not usually. Today it was only because—oh, you know—look, I will work on the kisses, really I will, the next time we rehearse them—"

He cut off her protests with one of those imperious gestures of his out-flung arm she remembered from her audition.

"The first kiss. The unexpected one. You've done it so often in rehearsal that you've completely lost the element of surprise. You find it hard to act startled because you know exactly what's coming. Whereas—"

Suddenly interrupting himself, Tor caught her face in both his hands and kissed her on the lips, releasing her instantly.

Utterly astonished, she stared at him, her mouth still open, hardly breathing, until he tapped her lightly on the shoulder.

"Very, very good. You see, you can do it."

Dazed, Marigold shook her head, feeling as if she had been thrown into ice-cold water. She stared at him, but he only smiled back in a way that made her senses reel.

"You felt the difference. It showed on your face. Get inside that feeling. Stay in the moment—be as large as you can in that urgent present. You must re-create it as fresh and new as that, every time."

Had that really happened? Had Tor just kissed her? He was expecting her to say something—but nothing clever or witty came, just her admission: "I totally was not expecting that."

"Of course you weren't, so in a way, we were cheating, but do you think you can remember that sensation next time?"

How could I forget it? thought Marigold. Not that it was a lingering or erotic kiss, but there was something larger than life about Tor that endowed his actions with a magic that was all his own.

He was pacing up and down the carpet now, wide-awake, full of vitality. Marigold began to feel trickles of excitement up and down her spine. Whatever would happen next?

"Now. Kiss number two, the passionate one, where it's Polly driving the action along, because she isn't flirting, she's giving all of herself to the man she's fallen in love with. Do you mind if I give you some advice? Please don't take this as a comment on your real life kissing technique, but in my experience, a stage kiss is vastly improved if you first let all the air out of your lungs. This relaxes the mouth and creates a wonderful impression of passion and sensuality. Watch Lydia—she has it to perfection."

"And what do I do?"

"You take a big breath in, as if you were about to blow out candles on a birthday cake—which is personally endearing, but it's too innocent for Polly; she's an adult, she knows exactly what she's doing. So, by all means keep doing that in your offstage romantic life. But for the play—shall we give it a go?"

He stood very still, arms by his sides, looking at her in an amused, questioning way.

This is ridiculous, thought Marigold. *He's standing there, waiting for me to try it. Is the play really the only thing on his mind? He's not making a move; he won't do anything unless I go to him. For the sake of the play, I should do it. (For myself...oh, I want to, but let's not go there). Let's do it!*

Acting confident, she went toward him, aware of the difference in height between them. He bent his head down to hers, and she let out a long, sighing breath.

"Perfect," he murmured as their lips met.

Tor's mouth was relaxed against hers, his lips softly molded to her own, but then, as they both drew breath, the kiss became fiercer, more urgent, hotter, and she felt his tongue teasing, flicking like a serpent into the hot desert of her mouth, making her liquid with desire in the secret parts of her intimate self.

Suddenly he lifted her up to his own height, whirled her around, and deposited her, breathless and almost laughing, on the infamous black satin sheets. Then, with infinite, teasing slowness, he drew his mouth away from hers.

They both lay there, gazing at each other in delight, surprise, and exhaustion. Marigold had a huge grin on her face, and Tor was shaking the bed with his immense, warm chuckle.

"That was some kiss," he said, "Now, do you think you can do it like that for me onstage?"

At that exact moment, the coffee arrived, and Tor tipped the boy lavishly, while Marigold tried unsuccessfully to look as if she was only lying on the bed for a rest. The bellboy gave her an enormous wink as he left.

They stayed there, resting on the pillows and sipping coffee until Marigold's taxi arrived.

Then Tor sprang up, helped her gather her things, and wished her goodnight, with nothing more than a friendly clasping of hands.

A moment later and she was whisked away into the night.

*

Afterwards, lying back in bed in the safe haven of her bedroom, Marigold, with her eyes closed, tried to remember each microsecond of that perfect kiss. Her tiredness had evaporated and her mind was busy with images and thoughts of Tor. How kind he had been to her. What fun, what certainty and confidence in his vision. She saw his face again, bent toward hers, and a delicious thrill of anticipation ran through her. Forget Barrie. She would be seeing Tor again tomorrow...and the next day...and the next.

CHAPTER SIX

Marigold approached the theatre next morning with a heart floating skyward like a hot air balloon. She almost skipped down the corridor, and, pushing open the door to the rehearsal room a little too vigorously, she collided with Brian Hancock, coming the other way.

"You really are frightfully athletic," he complained, as Marigold apologized and helped him pick up the contents of the carrier bag he had dropped on the floor. "Lucky for you, there was nothing breakable in there."

"I'm so sorry, really I am, Brian."

He gave her a cold look from his heavy features.

"How can I atone?" she asked. "What about buying you lunch?"

He looked a little shifty, and shook his head. "All is forgiven, dear girl. Lunch is not necessary. I have—ahem—another engagement."

Marigold made straight for the stage. It was empty and quiet, and she saw straight away that a few little extra touches had been added since the previous day—gold leaf had been skilfully applied to the mirror frame, and there was now a realistic-looking fire in the grate. Above her, all the lights were hooked onto the battens that ran the width of the stage. Once they were lit, she would no longer be able to see into the auditorium to pick out individual faces; instead, there would be a dark pool into which her lines would drop, creating, she hoped, ripples of applause or laughter.

Marigold caught sight of Don Burlington, with a steel measure in his hand. She greeted him with a cheery wave and smile, but he did not respond in kind. Instead, he beckoned her over to the wings.

"Did you do this?" he asked, rather accusingly. He pointed to the cloak, gloves, and hat where she had left them the day before, hanging on the useful piece of scenery.

"Yes, it's just the right place for me there—it's a bit far to go all the way to the props table," she said carelessly.

"It may be the right place for you, but it's exactly the wrong place for me and my crew," said Don, and she thought how grim his voice sounded. "Every time they run on to do a scene change, that cloak will get in the way, and if you're going to leave it there it will certainly get torn."

"Oh, bother." Marigold hated being made to feel small, but her good humor soon reasserted itself. "Okay, Don. I'll use the props table, I promise."

Don's serious expression vanished and he gave her a smile. "What a relief! I thought it might have been Lydia who'd left them there. If it was, I'd have got my balls bitten off."

Marigold was usually the first one to arrive, and today was no exception, but she didn't mind; it gave her more time to savor that delicious moment when Tor would arrive. He would burst through the door at the back of the stalls, calling the scene as he sat down and Jenny scuttled behind, ready with her notebook.

But ten o'clock came, and there was no one else there. No Tor, no Jenny, and no cast. Even Brian had disappeared. Marigold was baffled.

A few minutes later, Carol Davies found her sitting rather forlornly on Lady Sophie's chaise longue. "Ah—there you are. Found you at last. I tried texting you but I guess you don't bring your mobile with you to rehearsals?"

"No. Because Tor—"

"Mm, I know, he's banned them, he hates them—he's been known to drop them in boiling water. You're very wise."

"What's wrong? Where is everyone?"

Marigold's mind was working overtime—had Barrie walked out? Lydia got a better offer?

"Nothing too terrible, just a bit of a nuisance. Tor can't be here today. He's been called to London on urgent business. Everyone else is in my office—let's go and see what we can sort out."

Marigold's face fell. She wanted to sulk and stamp her foot. She had been so ready to give Tor her best, to amaze him with the improvement they had worked on last night, to earn his praise and his mesmerizing smile. How dare he not be there, when she wanted so much to see him.

As they made their way through the corridors, Marigold got no more information from the briskly efficient Carol.

They arrived at the office, where the atmosphere was tense. All the cast was there.

Lydia waved a lazy cigarette in Carol's direction. "It's a bitch, isn't it?" she drawled.

"Do you know why he had to go?" asked Marigold, acting very hard to sound only casually interested.

"Ohhh, we could have a guess. Couldn't we, people?" Lydia included the rest of the group with her knowing smirk, and they nodded or murmured.

Marigold was suddenly gripped with terror. "He hasn't left for good, has he? Not resigned?"

Lydia shook her head, her impossibly lustrous hair following the exquisite line of her neck and shoulders. She shook it back with loving impatience. "It's Blanche. Or Sandra. Or—who's the new one?"

"Cherchez la femme, indeed," murmured Brian, opening a toffee.

"You mean he's left rehearsals, not because of business but because of some—personal problems?" Marigold blurted out, aware of how prissy she sounded.

Lydia scarcely concealed a weary smile. "Women *are* his business."

"But that's so unprofessional—" Marigold's anger began to take control of her voice and to her horror, she was squeaking like a ten-year-old. Luckily, Barrie interrupted.

"Oh, for God's sake, everyone, let's leave it and do some work. Costume fittings or whatever. Carol—why don't you organize us?"

They drifted back to the theatre and Carol contacted David Trench, the company manager, to stand in for Tor. Jenny Warren could have run the rehearsal—she knew the moves and all the actors' lines by heart—but she was far too timid to handle personalities like Lydia's. Under David's intelligent eye, they ran the play and tried to bring it to life.

But Marigold had never realized until that moment what a huge contribution Tor made to the buzz and excitement of rehearsals. His unpredictability, his dizzying charm, and even his outbursts of temper had kept them on their toes; his energy and concentration had made them stretch and strain for perfection, to be rewarded with a smile, a nod, a word of approval. Without Tor, there was no point in giving that extra something.

Marigold went through the love scenes with Barrie with less than half her mind on the job. The kisses she had practised so memorably with Tor now became technical and lifeless.

Barrie attacked her during an extended tea break. (Without Tor to shout at them, all the breaks became extended—and Lydia even lit a cigarette in the rehearsal room.) "Are you happy? You've killed this play stone dead," Barrie raged at her. "And I've got friends coming from London to see this pantomime."

"So have I. And I am trying really hard, so don't pick on me, Barrie. You haven't exactly sparkled today."

"Damn Tor," was all he said in reply, and Marigold fervently agreed. Damn Tor! Surely he must realize the damage a whole day's absence would do at this crucial stage? Things were falling apart onstage, and the company morale offstage was as crumbly as a child's sandcastle on Branchester beach.

Lunch was an eternity in coming; when David eventually called a halt, Marigold felt she wanted to run away from the theatre and never see any of them again. As she left the building, her heart sank when she saw Helen Grant moving purposefully toward her, waving determinedly.

"Come on, I know a nice place where we can get away from the luvvies," said Helen, tucking her arm through Marigold's in a sisterly, bossy way. "I've had it up to here with bloated egos and neurotic overgrown kiddies."

They passed the baguette shop and went further into town. There would be no angry questions if they were ten minutes late getting back.

Helen was actively avoiding other members of the cast—when she saw Evelyn and Brian walking sedately past, she grabbed Marigold and hid behind a tree.

"Fancy that—Evelyn's got a toy boy!" sniggered Helen, steering her unwilling companion past the coffee shop where Tor had bought her that first cappuccino, through the Alleys, until they came to a rather tired-looking teashop.

"Best value in Branchester," boasted Helen. "You can order one pot of tea here, and they keep bringing you refills of hot water."

Marigold was too depressed to be hungry; she sat and waited as Helen organized baked beans on toast. She had clearly been planning this tête-à-tête for some time, so it would be just as well to get it over with.

With a sigh of satisfaction, Helen poured out tea for them both. "The little darlings are beginning to show their tiny fangs, n'est-ce pas?" she began, but Marigold interrupted her with a weary gesture.

"Sorry, Helen, but I don't want to get into a gossip session."

Helen gave a little jump of indignation. "Of course not. But you would like to know where Tor is, wouldn't you?"

Marigold felt like crying. Something awful was about to happen. "Where is he? You know something? Why didn't you say before?"

"Oh, I wasn't going to stick my neck out and get my head bitten off by Lydia, no thanks very much."

Helen began cutting up her baked beans and toast into tiny squares—an old dieter's trick, Marigold supposed. "The fact is, of course, that Lydia is in love with Tor, but he can't do anything because he's still horribly tangled up with Blanche."

"His—his wife."

Helen nodded eagerly. "In name—oh, but you know the story? You must have heard the story?"

"I don't know anything about Tor, except what he told me about being brought up in Glasgow—"

"Oh, he's given you the old 'born in a tenement' spiel, has he?" Helen laughed in a mirthless way. "Well, he has had the worst possible luck with all of his wives—why he bothered to get married to them all I can't imagine; they would have moved in with him at the flicker of an eyelash. But he's quite old-fashioned in some ways. Anyway, Blanche is still his current wife. But she's locked up."

"Locked up? You mean in prison?"

"Worse. Mental hospital. Sectioned."

Marigold pushed her plate of beans away untasted. "How awful. How terrible for him."

"Terrible for *her* that he put her there," said Helen, eyeing Marigold's lunch speculatively.

"What do you mean, he put her there?"

"Well, if it hadn't been for—oh, sod it!" Helen broke off as the café door swung open and Robin appeared.

"Ah, Helen—thought you'd be here. Carol says you won't be needed this afternoon; rehearsals are canceled."

"What about me?" asked Marigold.

Robin waggled his finger at her. "You'd better put your skates on and get back—they want you for costume fittings at two."

Robin downed a swift cup of tea and left. Helen ordered a teacake.

Marigold was putting on her coat to leave when Helen said, "You know the scene where you wanted to put in a little pausette? You were quite right, of course."

"Then why did Tor make me cut it?"

Helen gave her a frankly challenging look. "Because Lydia was putting pressure on him, of course. She's ruthless and she has to have the limelight. Twenty-four seven."

"I knew I was right!"

Helen dropped her voice to a stage whisper. "I'll tell you what to do. Do the scene as Tor told you, until the dress rehearsal. At the dress run, put back a tiny fraction of a pause. If Lydia and Tor don't notice, on the first night reinstate the pause, just as you did it. If the show's a huge success, as we know it will be, they'll both be too busy with the press and the bouquets and the fuss to say anything. And if Lydia says anything to you after that, just tell her you are doing it as rehearsed."

Marigold was shaken by the look of triumph on Helen's face. Almost as if this tiny victory would be hers too.

"You've acted with Lydia before, haven't you?"

"Yes, for my sins. It was the worst experience of my life. Just stay on her good side, is my advice."

"She's hardly noticed me," said Marigold.

"Oh, don't you fool yourself. She's noticed everything, from your voice to your smile to your hair to the one thing you have in spades that she hasn't—your youth. That's what she hates you for the most."

"She hates me?"

"Oh, don't listen to me. I'm a tired, bitter, not very successful actress who was never ruthless enough to clamber up the greasy ladder by treading on other people's faces."

"Oh, but Lydia didn't do that, surely—she has fabulous talent, that's what her success is based on," cried Marigold, realizing she was going to be at least fifteen minutes late for her fitting, but unable to leave, hypnotized by Helen.

"Whatever," sighed Helen. "But remember this. I know Lydia and I've seen the damage she can do. Watch your back. Never drop your guard."

It sounded as if she and Lydia were going to be in a boxing ring, not a theatre, thought Marigold as she jogged back to the theatre. And how horrible to hear all Tor's secrets; fascinating though they were, it wasn't fair of Helen to tell those intimate details to someone she hardly knew.

It was a welcome change to be fussed over by Tina and Peggy. They made minute adjustments to her costume, although she thought it quite perfect already, and beamed delightedly as she exclaimed with pleasure, twirling in front of the long mirror. Tina had even made an invisible little pocket in the side of her apron to slip some of her props into.

Flattered by her compliments and interest, they showed her all the other costumes, including Lady Sophie's exquisite peach satin ball gown, decorated with seed pearls, all sewn on by hand.

Tina was in a happy, excited mood; she told Marigold she had just moved house and was having a friend round for a housewarming dinner.

Marigold felt a twinge of envy. Steak and wine and a new house, a steady job doing what she was good at, and probably a nice boyfriend somewhere...

Walking home, Marigold gave herself a good talking to, remembering her forceful words to Betsy about her career and her ambitions. *You don't want any attachments yet, my girl*, she told herself. *The last thing you need is to be lumbered with a house and a boyfriend.*

But suddenly she thought about Tor in London, visiting his tragic wife, and life took on a bleak and flinty aspect.

*

Tor was back the next morning, and by the time the cast arrived, he had evidently been hard at work for some hours. The stage crew was gathered around him with schedules and Jenny was frantically making notes. Don Burlington was deep in conversation with Martin, the stage manager, and Steve the chief electrician.

Tor dismissed them all briskly and turned his attention to the cast. "Okay, this is the plan. Today: tech run, tops and tails, full tech run. Tomorrow—dress run, no stops, no tech. Friday—press and photo call, then full dress with tech. My apologies for my absence yesterday—it was unavoidable."

These words were greeted with either horror or anger from all the actors. A tech run! No time to make up for the lost day's rehearsal! They surely weren't ready?

Lydia strode across to Tor with battle in her eyes. "Rather a lame apology, wouldn't you say?"

He stood his ground. "I'm not wasting everyone's time with futile explanations."

"If you think we are ready for a tech run, you have another think coming," purred Lydia.

Everyone, cast and stage crew, had fallen silent. They watched and waited to see who would win this battle of the titans.

Marigold's heart was in her mouth as Tor's eyes moved from one mutinous face to another. She wanted him to win this fight—but in her gut and in her nerves she felt that Lydia was right. How was he going to resolve this?

Tor took a step toward Lydia. His eyes fixed hers. "If I didn't know you were an artist to your fingertips—" he took her hand lightly, brushing those long fingers with his lips "—I would say you were scared, Lydia. Surely that isn't possible?"

His voice was warm, like dark honey poured over ice cream. Marigold felt herself melting, her will shaping itself to Tor's will, her trust in him absolute.

Lydia shifted her weight, disconcerted. She did not take her hand away. Finally, she dropped her gaze and Tor gently let go of her hand. He slowly looked around at each of the actors, speaking with passion, with conviction.

"This play. This performance. I know it's there. I've seen it, I've felt it. And so have you, each and every one of you."

Yes, he was looking at her now, and Marigold wanted to leap up, shout, sing, or roll over and over in front of him.

"One day's rehearsal will not rescue a bad piece. This is not a bad piece. I am working with the best, and you are giving of your best."

Why had he not become an actor? Marigold wondered. His presence, his authority, his eyes, his voice—he could have broken hearts with those gifts.

Suddenly, his poise and passion left him, and he stood in a pose of uncertainty and vulnerability. "And I am, with all my heart, sorry that I had to abandon you yesterday."

Lydia flung her arms around him and held him for a curiously charged moment.

Tor simply stood, receiving the hug, his arms by his sides.

Marigold's heart ached. How she longed to have the courage and confidence to do the same as Lydia.

Everyone breathed out as Lydia turned, her anger utterly dissolved, replaced by a smiling radiance. "What are we waiting for?" she asked her fellow actors. "The man says tech run—let's do a tech run."

The tension in the theatre snapped like breaking elastic, and in a moment there was a babble of voices and a scurrying of bodies as everyone took up their positions. Tor and Jenny went into the auditorium, Jenny holding her stopwatch at the ready.

Tor was back, and everything would be all right.

"Okay, everyone, this is for time. No stops unless there is utter catastrophe. And whatever the crew gets up to, I want total concentration from the cast. You may think I'm watching the lights, but I'm not. I am watching each and every one of you. So, let's go."

Marigold felt for the first time the exhilarating heat of the full stage lights illuminating her and the set. There was a buzz of energy crackling in the air. Lydia glided onto the stage and took up her position gracefully, not looking at Marigold as she sank gracefully onto the chaise longue. She never looked at Marigold before the play started.

A moment later came the exotic whisper of "Go tabs" from Don—the cue to press the button which electronically operated the heavy red stage curtains. Marigold heard the soft hum of power as the curtain slid smoothly upwards. In front of her was an immense pit of blackness. And somewhere in that pit was Tor.

*

Whether it was the effect of the lights, Tor's return, or simply the mounting excitement with the closeness of the first night, Marigold did not know, but from her first line, she felt Polly wriggle into delicious life, fizzing in her veins like champagne. Now she understood what Tor had meant by having fun with the character as she felt Polly creep under her skin and into her voice and gestures; she no longer saw Lydia and Barrie, but Lady Sophie and Lord Harcourt. When it came to the dreaded love scene, the first kiss really did take her by surprise, and with the second, she gave herself with dizzying abandon to Lord Harcourt.

The same energy seemed to possess them all. Even Evelyn, whose performance so far had been disappointing, became positively waspish as the bullying grandmother.

It did not matter that they were not wearing costumes or makeup; it did not matter that, in between the scenes, Don and his crew were sweating and swearing as they struggled with the complicated changes; it did not matter that there was no other audience because, with a surge of excitement, Marigold realized that it was Tor's presence alone that had brought enchantment and made the play come alive.

By the time she came to her final scene, the letter scene, she was so wrought up that when Lady Sophie dismissed her, the tears began to roll down her face. She made her exit still weeping, sobbing, but as soon as she was offstage, she felt as if she had won a race, and she began laughing and crying at the same time, trying to calm her beating heart. To her surprise, Marigold felt hands patting her shoulders, whispers of "well done" and "brilliant," and Tina handed her a glass of water, which she drank down in one gulp.

Finally it was all over, and the cast joined hands for a bow to the empty auditorium. As they straightened up, smiling into the darkness, they were rewarded by deep, sonorous handclaps from where Tor was sitting, and his voice sounded through the stalls with one word: "Bravo."

The cast went backstage to the green room to take a quick coffee break while Tor gave his notes to the stage crew, and suddenly the mood was effervescent. Smiles were on every face and there was a sudden injection of confidence as, for the first time, they all shared the unforgettable joy of live theatre at its best.

"Knockout," said Barrie to Marigold, and she was comfortably able to respond, "And you were terrific." Everyone hugged and kissed her—even Lydia, calling her "dear little Polly." Evelyn lay on the sofa while Brian gently fanned her with the chiffon scarf. Then Jenny arrived and summoned them all back onstage for director's notes. Marigold found that she was once again trembling with excitement. Would Tor have noticed her performance?

Everyone watched him anxiously as he sprawled in Lady Sophie's armchair, consulting his notes. Then he looked up, seeing their nervous expressions, and with perfect timing, grinned widely. "Well done."

Marigold felt a warm shiver of delight as his eyes rested on her, including her in the general praise.

"I'll say a brief word to each of you about your performance before we go through scene by scene..."

As he focused on each actor, he found something special to say about each, letting them know that there was nothing that had escaped his attention.

Finally, last of all, he turned to Marigold. "What a transformation!" he said, and she felt herself sinking into those dark eyes. "But have you anything left to give us for the first night?"

"Oh, yes—I hope so, yes," said Marigold fervently.

He tapped his pen on his script. "Only one note. The torrent of tears was a little OTT, wouldn't you agree? A waterfall might drown us all—and the audience."

Marigold joined in the friendly laughter that greeted this comment—her weeping had gone out of control, but it had been a wonderful feeling to be so moved.

Tor was still looking at her, on his face a grin of—pride? Affection? Pleasure, at any rate.

"I see my cruelty and nagging in rehearsal paid off," he continued, turning to Barrie. "The kissing scene was natural and spontaneous and lovely. Only one word of warning." He turned back to Marigold. "You mustn't be disappointed if it doesn't happen like that every time. You see, today we were all blessed with the magic that comes when we least expect it. We can encourage it with hard work and technique, we can humbly pray for it, and we can recognize it when we see it in others. It's that elusive, frustrating ecstasy that keeps us in this bloody, awful, cruel profession that in so many ways can be so saddening and heartbreaking."

Marigold drank in every word, her energy suddenly taut as a bowstring. He was right. He was right about everything.

Her reverent mood was abruptly ripped apart, however, after Tor had finished giving notes and dismissed everyone for lunch. She could not help watching as he strolled over to Lydia.

"Will you come to lunch with me?"

"Of course."

Lydia leaned close to him, and Marigold saw his eyes hold hers with their unsettling, passionate intensity.

"My dear. Thank you for trusting me," he said softly.

Lydia lifted her slim hand to stroke the thick, wiry waves of black hair from Tor's high forehead. Then she brushed his cheek with a kiss. Her voice was low and thrilling. "You know perfectly well you can do anything you want with me," she murmured languorously, and Marigold, feeling angry and embarrassed, slid from the room.

All her excitement and sense of achievement evaporated in an instant, and was replaced by inexplicable irritation. This was aggravated by almost running into Helen outside the green room. Helen was looking pleased with herself.

"What did I tell you?" She hissed in Marigold's ear, making her jump. "She's crazy for him."

"But—he loves his wife..." The words were dragged out of her.

Helen looked slyly satisfied. "Yes, but people change, don't they? Especially in this business. And he has just asked her to lunch—hasn't he?"

CHAPTER SEVEN

With Tor's return, everything at the theatre seemed under control once more, and the blissful mood of co-operation amongst the cast lasted for the whole of the next day. Tor even managed to make time to run through any scenes they were unhappy with—but somehow, they all felt confident now, ready to face a real audience.

The day of the dress rehearsal was sunny but cold, and Marigold relished the luxury of a morning in bed, catching up on Facebook and emails, reading magazines, and occasionally checking her script whenever last minute nerves attacked her. Tor had called the dress run for three o'clock, but by two, Marigold could no longer keep away from the theatre. The charms of sunshine, Branchester, and the beach were no rivals to the dark, fragrant, excitement-laden atmosphere of the stage and its glittering set.

She went to the rehearsal room and did half an hour of physical and vocal warming up; today she was alone, and she relished it. Hurrying downstairs to the dressing room she shared with Helen, she took out her box of "slap" and began to apply the pungent greasepaint.

Suddenly, the door burst open and Helen burst in, her face a tragic mask. "You'll never guess what's happened!"

"What now?"

Marigold had no time for scandal-mongering today.

"It's Evelyn; she's had some sort of breakdown. She's not coming in for the dress run!"

"Oh, no!" gasped Marigold, horrified. She had some important scenes with the old lady. Anyway, how could they run the play with a character missing? "Are you sure this is true, Helen?"

"Absolutely. Carol Davies told me. Apparently Evelyn's landlady rang in to say she's in bed, too ill to move."

"And what does Tor say?"

Helen sat down and opened her greasepaints with a sniff. "He's postponed the press call because he wants Evelyn in it."

"Helen, how can you just sit there so calmly?"

"Because it's only a rehearsal. It's not a real show. Save the histrionics for the first night."

"There may not be a first night! We might have to—"

She was interrupted by a brisk tapping on the door. She sprang up and opened it. Tor stood on the threshold, on his face an expression that Marigold could not fathom.

"I have to tell you that, sadly, Evelyn is not well," he said, staring down at the floor, "and she will not be in for the dress run. Jenny will read in for her."

He looked up, standing in that uncertain pose he had taken when he was apologizing. Then Marigold remembered Lydia flinging herself at him, and any sympathy she may have had for his difficulties as director melted away.

But he was still standing there, and she could not help meeting his gaze.

"I appreciate that this will make your task this afternoon far harder than you expected, but I hope your sympathy for a fellow artiste who is under great strain, and your own professionalism, will carry you through. I'll see you after the run. Oh, and good luck."

He went away, leaving Marigold's thoughts spinning. How many scenes did she have with Lady Trensham? Not many, thank goodness. Poor Lydia—some of her most important scenes would be ruined today. And what about tomorrow? Jenny could hardly read in for the first night. All the London papers would be there!

Her thoughts were interrupted by Helen, who was carefully applying a large black beauty spot to one cheek. "He should never have hired her, of course."

"Why on earth did he, if she's so flaky?"

Helen gave her an amused look. "Because once upon a time,

when he was a wee boy, he saw a great actress playing Hedda Gabler, and he's such a sentimental fool, he never got over it."

"Don't you trust his judgement, then?" said Marigold. "He always seems so super-confident."

Helen smiled at her own corpse-white powdered face, high wig, and crimson lips with great satisfaction. She looked good, thought Marigold, very good—haughty and aristocratic, a perfect foil for the innocent Lady Sophie.

"My dear, it's all an act! At this very moment, he's probably wetting his knickers, glugging back the whisky and crying on Jenny's shoulder."

The image conjured up by these carelessly delivered words was unbearable. Marigold stood up, hurriedly pulling on her cap.

"I have to go. I'll be back in a minute."

She escaped from the dressing room, the picture of Tor that Helen had conjured up ringing horribly true. Of course, the responsibility for hiring Evelyn was entirely Tor's. If she was not equal to the challenge, the blame would fall on him. His reputation was hanging by a thread.

Marigold hurried along the corridor toward the stage. She did not know what she was going to do, only that she had to find Tor, had to help him, if she could. The idea of that strong face, wet with tears, moved and at the same time appalled her. If he was crying, she wanted to be the shoulder his head rested on.

But when she found him, he was far from the heap of misery Helen had depicted. He was leaning against a ladder by the stage, laughing and chatting to Don and Tina. They looked surprised to see her.

"Have you been called already?" asked Tor. "Don't we have another ten minutes before we go up?"

Don checked his phone. "Nine and a half."

"I was looking for you, Tor," said Marigold. "I wanted to offer my help, if it's of any use. Maybe Evelyn needs some extra help with her lines or something."

"Thank you, that's very generous." Tor thought for a moment, raking the unruly hair back from his forehead, and Marigold noticed the lines of strain settle around his mouth and eyes. Then his face crinkled into a smile. "There are two things you could do. One is to find Jenny, who's probably hiding in the green room shaking with nerves, and give her a bit of sisterly support. Standing on a stage reading lines is a nightmare for her, so if you could cheer her up that would be wonderful. The second thing...wait, come with me."

He led her away from Don and Tina to a dark corner backstage and looked at her hard, holding her arm with a strong grip. "You don't have to do this. Can I rely on you to be discreet?"

"Yes, of course."

Tor bit his lip, let go of her arm, and rested one hand on her shoulder. "I must go and talk to Evelyn as soon as we finish. Would you come with me?"

Marigold's voice was squeaky with surprise. "Me? Why?"

"I know Evelyn can do this part—will do it tomorrow, and will do it as no other actor could. Believe me, she is a great, great actor. Greater even than Lydia, in her heyday. But what destroys her is a devil standing at her elbow, telling her she is no good. She has a poisonous lack of self-esteem, in spite of trunks full of press reviews and newspaper cuttings and a stage career of more than fifty years. I daresay she even feels inferior to you."

"Oh, surely not, I'm so inexperienced and ignorant and new to it all—"

"Yes, yes, you're all those things. But you have youth, and fire, and a joy in what you do. Evelyn only sees what she doesn't have. Come with me; you can convince her that we need her."

Marigold must have looked doubtful, for he suddenly tightened his grip on her shoulder. "If you won't come for her sake, come for mine. I'm asking you to come with me. I want you there with me."

His words, whispered with such a passion, aroused in Marigold a painful and sweet longing—to lift her hand to his head and stroke back his hair, as Lydia had done, and then to kiss him...on the cheek, as she had done—

In the darkness, she felt herself blushing. "Of course I'll come," she whispered back.

"Thank you."

If he was going to say more, it was interrupted by Lydia, Brian, and Robin trooping past in their costumes. Five minutes to go. Tor quietly disappeared. Marigold ran to find Jenny.

*

The old theatrical cliché says a bad dress rehearsal means a perfect first night. By this token, everyone in the Tower Theatre Company should have been delightedly anticipating a stunningly successful performance the next day.

It was a disaster from start to finish. Everyone had a crisis. Brian stumbled on the carpet, falling heavily, and the scene had to be stopped so he could be checked for fractures or a sprained ankle. Then Lydia entered by the wrong door and fluffed her lines. Don's crew moved the wrong scenery after the first scene, so the cast unexpectedly found themselves in Lady Sophie's garden. Polly, wrestling with a stuck door, found the handle had come away in her hand and burst into nervous giggles. Jenny, reading in for Lady Trensham, spoke in a tiny voice, pulling her hair across her face and not meeting anyone's eyes. And Robin, as the footman, dropped a full tea-tray onstage, breaking two of the hired teacups.

Throughout this painful fiasco, Tor sat silent. He left the cast and crew to get themselves out of trouble—in performance, that was what they were going to have to do.

Marigold longed to hear his voice, even raised in anger—for the uncharacteristic silence from the auditorium seemed extremely ominous.

Finally, the ordeal was over and the cast joined hands and faced the rows of empty seats. The radiant smiles of two days ago were replaced by haunted looks of apprehension, as if they were expecting rotten tomatoes and eggs to come their way.

Then, a shout from Tor: "Smile, for God's sake! Play it to the hilt! This was the best night of your lives! Make me believe it! ACT IT!"

Under the spell of his personality, they did.

There were no notes afterwards, only the time of their call tomorrow—and a gentle word of reassurance.

"This hasn't been the worst dress run I've ever seen," Tor began lightly, "but I'd say it comes close. Go home and get an early night. And, all of you, don't worry. Because I won't."

"What about Evelyn?" asked Lydia.

"Evelyn will be here tomorrow. I promise."

The cast straggled back to their dressing rooms. Marigold and Helen took off their makeup and changed out of their costumes. For once, Helen did not have a word to say.

Marigold was soon ready, and went to find Tor, who was sorting out technical problems with a very apologetic Don. Once again, Marigold marveled at Tor's ability to give his concentrated attention to one person, to the exclusion of everything else. She stood quietly, waiting till he had finished and Don had taken the stage crew off for a pint and a pep talk. Then he smiled at her.

"Come on, Miss Mouse."

He held out his hand, and she took it, feeling as if they were old friends. Together they walked through the corridors to the open air. Tor's thoughts must have been only of Evelyn, not of her, and Marigold was simply happy to be walking beside him.

As soon as they were outside, Marigold realized how tired she was. And, seeing Tor's face in the late afternoon sunlight, how exhausted he was too. He hailed a taxi, gave the driver Evelyn's address, and lay back, staring out of the window with a faraway look on his face.

Evelyn's digs were in a neglected-looking Edwardian house at the unfashionable end of the seafront, almost out of town. The small front garden was overgrown with weeds and a straggling, dusty privet hedge.

They rang the bell and waited. Finally, a bald man in slippers and a beige cardigan shuffled to the door.

"The old lady? First floor."

The house was pervaded by the smell of boiled cabbage, and the paint on the walls was peeling. Marigold went up the uncarpeted stairs, feeling her anger mounting. Old lady, indeed! How dare they treat her like this!

Evelyn's room was large and bare, with a sagging double bed squeezed next to an ugly old wardrobe and a cheap chest of drawers. The windows were grimy, framed with tattered lace curtains, looking out onto a back yard. Two rough squares of carpet were tacked together on the floor, leaving dangerous gaps that Evelyn could easily have tripped over.

She was sitting up in bed, dressed in a faded pink satin bed-jacket. There were dark circles under her eyes. As soon as she saw Tor, Evelyn began to cry in a quiet, humiliated way. She tried to smile, but the tears flowed down her cheeks. Tor sat on the bed and took her hand. He waited until she had recovered her dignity, then gave her the gentlest of hugs.

"Would you like a cup of tea?" asked Marigold.

"I don't like to bother them. I feel I'm being such a nuisance to everyone," mumbled Evelyn, dabbing her eyes with one of her chiffon scarves.

"You need some tea, we all do. Don't you worry, I'll get some."

Marigold found the kitchen, and under the lackluster eye of the slippered man made a pot of tea. He made a feeble protest when Marigold picked out the best china, but she ignored him and carried the tray upstairs, her temper barely under control.

"Oh, how good you are," said Evelyn as the tears threatened to overwhelm her yet again. Marigold poured her a cup and put sugar in, hoping it would give Evelyn some energy.

"This is shameful! Evelyn, I don't know what to say—" Marigold could not hide her anger any longer.

Evelyn nodded sadly. "I know. I have to accept that I am really too old to work anymore," she said quietly. "I am so sorry to have let you all down."

"That's not what I meant!" cried Marigold. "And you haven't let us down. We all made the most awful mistakes today—you would have laughed if you'd seen us, honestly you would. I'm just furious that you are living here, in this dreadful place. Someone with your reputation ought to be treated with more respect. You deserve better."

"I agree," said Tor. "You are coming to stay at the Sovereign with me. Don't argue—you'll come, if I have to carry you there myself."

"Oh, but the cost—" protested Evelyn, but he waved this aside.

"The company will pay. This place isn't fit to house a rat."

"There aren't any rats here, at least," said Evelyn, looking more cheerful.

"That proves my point. Even a rat has more sense than to live here."

"You are too kind, but I think it would be better if you were to find someone else to be Lady Trensham."

Tor took Evelyn's hand. "Hedda Gabler. Remember this—all the years, all the roles, all the talents you have, everything that goes to make you Evelyn de Laurier."

Evelyn's thin hands plucked at the ribbon of her bed-jacket. "I don't have the same courage these days. I knew when I woke up this morning that, after suffering the ordeal of the rehearsals, the performance would be quite, quite beyond me."

Her voice sounded lifeless and resigned. Marigold, who had

been perched on a rickety chair by the window, suddenly leapt to her feet.

"What about the day of the tech run? Have you forgotten how the play came to life then? How excited we all were, how happy? And that long speech of yours, that wonderful speech, how you were able to put years of experience and disillusion and sadness into those words? I totally believed in you, you *were* Lady Trensham. I missed you today, I missed you terribly. Please, please come back, Evelyn."

"I will stake my reputation on your performance tomorrow," Tor said as he got up to go.

"You aren't alone, you know," said Marigold, kissing her wrinkled cheek and giving her a hug.

She was so frail, so faded. Yet Tor believed in her. She must begin to believe in herself.

"I'll do my best. If you think I can do it, I'd better get on with the show," she said, beginning to twinkle a little.

"Thank you for trusting me," said Tor.

Marigold drew in her breath sharply as she remembered when she had last heard that phrase. He had said it to Lydia—and it had been followed by a caress and a kiss.

Leaving Tor to sort out transfer arrangements for Evelyn, Marigold was glad to leave the gloomy house, but when she reached the gate, she hesitated. Part of her wanted to escape the complicated feelings Tor aroused in her—but in another part of her was a stronger, savage longing which threatened to overwhelm her with its wild sweetness. She wanted to be alone with Tor—wanted whatever excitement, risk or even danger that would bring. As she stood, uncertain, Tor came leaping down the front steps to stand by her side.

"Let's walk a while, shall we?" he suggested. "I need some fresh air after the horrors of that vile place."

He strode along while Marigold almost had to run to keep up with him, till he slowed down with a grin and an apologetic shrug.

"Have you any idea how old she is?" he asked as they stopped to look at the lights of the little pier winking in the early sunset.

"Oh, seventy something? It's hard to tell."

"Eighty-one. When she began her career, she was fifteen—younger than you. The stage was lit by gaslights that were so hot the actors' greasepaint melted and ran down their faces. The curtain was raised by a man turning a giant wheel by hand—and television hadn't been invented."

"No wonder she's terrified."

"Not like you. Full of fight and with an answer for everything."

"Sometimes a kiss takes me unawares." She watched his face break into a smile as they both remembered the evening in his room, which now seemed light years away. Then he turned away, looking out to sea.

"Marigold..."

"What?"

He leaned against the sea wall, burying his face in his hands for a brief moment. Then he straightened up, drawing a cloak over his feelings, and the unspoken thing between them vanished away.

"Nothing. Or rather—something, but this is not the time."

His face was granite now, curiously hard, yet she could not help staring at him, longing to hear what he would say next.

"I wonder how long it will take you to become bruised by life. I hope you never lose your shine." The words were reluctant, and Marigold willed him to go on speaking.

Suddenly he sprang to the top of the sea wall and held his hand out to her.

"Come." She took his hand and he pulled her up as easily as if she were a child. They stood together hand in hand on the wall, and Marigold had only the briefest moment to look down and register the drop of seven feet to the beach below before he was jumping down, pulling her with him, and they fell on the sandy shingle, laughing and breathless.

Tor helped her up and went on toward the distant waves, stooping to fill his hands with flat beach pebbles. Marigold followed, watching as he leaned back, flicked his arm and sent the stone skimming along the wavelets. Seven, no, eight bounces. He skimmed another and another, then offered one to Marigold. Hers sank.

"What's the secret?"

"Practice. Come here."

He stood just behind her, putting a stone into her hand. Then, with his hand closed over hers, he showed her the angle, moved her arm back, then forward. As she let go, she had the satisfaction of watching it bounce three or four times.

"Make a wish," said Tor. "When it's your first time, you get to make a wish."

They turned back toward the town; Tor, seeming calmer, strolled with his hands in his pockets, relaxed yet absent. Marigold felt a cool breeze blowing off the sea, and her exhilaration drained away as the street lights flickered into life. They came to the point where their paths went in different directions.

"Would you like me to walk you home?" he asked, but she shook her head. Her moment had passed—his thoughts were of Evelyn, of tomorrow, certainly not of her.

"No, I'm fine."

He seemed about to speak, but only reached out and took both her hands in his. In spite of the cold, his hands were warm.

"Thanks for what you did back there. See you tomorrow."

And he was gone.

*

Saturday—First Night Day, as Marigold saw it, with capital letters—began with the insistent beeping of her phone. Struggling awake, she saw she had missed a call from Betsy, who was due to arrive that afternoon. She'd left a breathless voicemail: "Sorry, really sorry, can't make it, I've had a call for an audition, God, so exciting, I have to go now, call you later, massive good luck tonight darling and if you can, spare a thought for me at two-thirty!"

So Betsy wouldn't be there tonight. Nor would her parents, as they couldn't leave the shop at the weekend. They would be there on Monday. Tonight there would be no one in the audience especially there for her.

"Oh well, good thing really, in case everything goes wrong. No one will know," she was telling herself—then, with a terrified quiver, she remembered the press would be there.

And Tor would be there.

She was sitting at the breakfast table, feeling rather sorry for herself, when Mrs. Harbour bustled in. She laid out Marigold's breakfast, then presented her with three tiny roses done up as a buttonhole.

"To wear afterwards, it's quite a tradition at the Tower," she said. "Oh, and I'll be there. I go to all the first nights. I'll be watching out for you particularly, and I'll clap for all your good bits."

After breakfast, the day seemed to stretch endlessly ahead. They were not called until seven. Marigold did not know what to do with herself; she wanted to be in the theatre, then she wanted to be anywhere but there; she wanted to see Tor, then she dreaded seeing him. She wanted the play to be over, and the next minute, she didn't ever want the curtain to rise on the first night. And there were hours and hours of this torture to endure!

It was raining steadily, so she put on her waterproof and set off for a walk. Maybe fresh air would clear her head and give her some courage.

Without thinking, she found herself walking back along the way she had walked with Tor last night, along by the shore. She clambered up on to the wall and looked down at the drop, amazed that she had had the nerve to jump. But Tor had been there; Tor had held her hand. Tor had believed she could do it. She almost groaned aloud, so sudden and strong was the pang of missing him.

"But when I do see him, I've got no way of knowing whether he'll be wonderful and adorable, or cold and furious, or just blank me out," she mused as she gathered flat stones and walked to the water's edge. "Perhaps he'll have had another catastrophe in his personal life and he won't even be there!" That thought was too awful to consider; Marigold began skimming stones with fierce concentration.

"Don't fool yourself, girl," she said aloud. "You're gagging to see him again, you know you are—whatever mood he's in."

Every stone sank without even one bounce.

Slowly, unbearably slowly, the day dragged on. The rain was persistent. Marigold saw a few bedraggled holidaymakers— families in waterproofs, trying to find wet weather activities. She bought a roll and a cup of tea from one of the kiosks on the seafront and ate and drank sitting in a bus shelter, watching the waves. Then, having exhausted all the activities Branchester had to offer, she went back to her digs.

As soon as she got up to her room, she realized to her surprise that she was sleepy. She went to bed and slept heavily until the alarm woke her. As she opened her eyes, the first wave of nervousness attacked her physically—a swimming sensation in the belly, and a sudden pounding of her heart. A moment later it was gone, but Marigold knew that it would return now at regular intervals, each time a little stronger, until, just before the curtain went up, she would be trembling with excitement, nausea, and terror. Of course, afterwards this panic would be forgotten. The rewards of applause and praise would cancel it out.

"But suppose it doesn't work tonight?" she asked her reflection in the bathroom mirror. "Suppose it's a total flop? Or, worse, suppose everyone else is brilliant, and I'm rubbish?" These and other unhelpful thoughts went chasing round and round in her head, up to the moment she entered the theatre building.

Walking to her dressing room, she met Evelyn. They both stopped. Marigold gasped. Evelyn giggled. Her hair was cut in a new style, the lines on her face were smoothed away, and she sported a beautifully cut cream linen suit, with a pink carnation in her buttonhole.

"What a glorious day I've had!" she sang. "I had my first ever Jacuzzi! And Tor sent a young woman to my room—a masseuse—and she sent me off to sleep in bliss with her healing hands. Then the hairdresser did this—what do you think?"

"Oh, Evelyn—what a transformation! You look wonderful!"

"Well, I have you and Tor to thank. I must dash, and so must you. See you on the green!"

Marigold felt such a sense of relief that Evelyn was present, cheerful, and prepared to perform, that it hardly mattered whether she gave a good performance or not.

"Let's just get through it," she muttered as she opened the door of her dressing room.

"Couldn't agree more," said Helen, who was already sitting in front of her mirror, looking pale. She rummaged in her bag for her lucky rabbit's foot, which she ritually kissed three times before hanging it on the mirror. She then produced an extremely old envelope, removed from it an ancient card with good luck wishes, and propped it up next to the rabbit's foot. Finally she stood up, turned around three times and sat down again.

"There. Good luck is now guaranteed."

"Will it work for me too?" wondered Marigold. "I hope so."

As they were putting the finishing touches to their slap, there was a gentle tap on the door. Marigold opened it, but there was no one there, only a huge bunch of white carnations, with both their names on the card.

The message said, *To two gorgeous girls—let's give it everything we've got.*

"Who would they be from?"

"Oh, Barrie. It's his kind of flashy taste, don't you think? Look at the red heart he's drawn with lipstick."

"Not from anyone else, then?"

"Tor never sends flowers before a show—he thinks they're unlucky."

Helen put the flowers in water while Marigold wondered if it was true that confident Tor could be superstitious.

"No, he'll take everyone out for a meal afterwards—and watch to see if he drinks. That would be a very bad sign."

Helen began powdering herself and her wig, and Marigold moved away from the fragrant clouds; she didn't want to be attacked by a fit of coughing onstage. There were only a few minutes to go. Ready now, and trembling with nerves, they hugged and wished each other luck.

A tinny voice came over the intercom: "Director's speech, one minute. Act One beginners, stand by."

Oh, of course, thought Marigold, *the director's speech*. How long would it be? How could her nerves stand it, waiting backstage as Tor sang the praises of the theatre, the company, and this particular production? Bugger tradition! Why did he have to speak before the play?

Marigold was taking deep breaths and trying to calm herself down as she waited in the wings. Suddenly, Tor was there in front of her.

"Is my tie straight?"

He'd never worn a tie in rehearsals. Marigold tentatively put up her hands and straightened it.

He was wearing a navy blue suit—just slouchy enough to be fashionable—with a pale blue shirt and a jade green velvet tie, and his eyes were sparkling and full of mischief.

"Oh—you're not quite perfect yourself," he said, and with infinite gentleness he tucked a stray tendril of hair under her maid's cap. For a long moment they stood, locked in a look that Marigold wished would last forever.

"Break a leg," he said to her, and was gone, out onto the stage and parting the curtains to greet the audience. A round of applause met his entrance.

The cast could hear the speech on the backstage intercom. If he was nervous, he didn't show it. His voice was deep, fascinating, and beautifully modulated. And he was by turns witty, modest, and fired with passion for this theatre, this company, this play. He had the audience in the palm of his hand. Marigold imagined him standing as he had stood in rehearsals—head flung back, legs slightly apart, one hand in his pocket, the other gesturing, emphasizing. His first joke was greeted with gales of laughter—which told the cast that the house was packed, not one seat empty.

Marigold didn't know whether that made her feel better or far worse; if she bombed tonight, she would be failing in front of hundreds of spectators. "Never forget your audience," Barrie had said. As if she could!

Finally the speech was over. More applause, and Tor would be stepping lightly down from the stage and going to take his seat among the audience. From now on, it was all up to them.

Marigold was onstage, hardly knowing how she got there, breathing deeply, concentrating on letting Polly inhabit her. Lydia glided on, sat on the chaise, and took up her embroidery. The lights came up, and just before the curtains rose, Lady Sophie smiled at Polly, and gave her a deliciously swift wink.

"Go tabs."

And they were off.

*

The performance went by in a blur, though a pleasant one. From the first chuckles to the torrent of applause that greeted the final curtain, it was a steadily rising curve of excitement, punctuated by sudden flashes of vivid detail. The scene with Lady Trensham was one of those moments. Evelyn had transformed herself: her thin face was stark white with vivid dots of scarlet high on her cheekbones and a pointed witch's chin. Her steely blue eyes fixed Polly with uncanny brilliance. From the first line of the scene, it was obvious who was in control. Polly began fetching and carrying, hearing the hearty laughter inspired by the acid commentary of the old lady. Lady Trensham knew how to take a laugh, when to roll her eyes, and when to do a double take. The audience laughed constantly. As Polly bent down to search for a fan, she heard a ripple of anticipatory chuckling. What was Lady Trensham up to now? The next minute, a pillow thrown, unrehearsed, by her, hit Polly neatly on her behind—but when she turned to face her, the old lady was demurely sitting in her bed, drinking tea, her eyes raised to heaven.

The audience obviously adored Lady Trensham, and as the scene came to an end, Marigold's only worry was that the comedy would unbalance the drama of the story.

Then came the kisses with Lord Harcourt. The first one, the surprise, was greeted with an "ooh" of excitement, and the second kiss provoked a sigh of satisfaction that rose from the audience like the breath of a mighty whale. Barrie's kiss was well above standard—but as Marigold closed her eyes, it was not his face that she saw.

The first interval found her sitting in her dressing room, tingling with adrenaline, longing for the next half. But there was a bunch of flowers by her mirror—marigolds.

"Helen, do you know—"

"No idea."

Marigold put them in water. Could Tor...no, he never gave flowers. He would be in the bar now, surrounded by admiring patrons, charming them all.

Jenny Warren put her head round the door with a message. "Tor says it's going like a rocket—keep up the energy."

Standing in the wings waiting for the second half to begin, Marigold saw Tina joined by Don, who slipped his arm round her shoulders and kissed the tip of her nose.

Bizarrely, seeing this made Marigold feel like crying.

The second half of the play saw the pace increase as light comedy gave way to passion, intrigue, and tragedy. Lady Trensham's long speech about her unrequited love was magnificent. Polly's eyes were prickling with tears as she tucked the old lady up in bed. Tor had been right—Evelyn was a great actress. He was always right.

And the love scene between Lord Harcourt and Lady Sophie, when they enumerate each other's faults in a scene of bantering comedy that turns to naked passion had the audience on the edge of their seats. As Barrie and Lydia came offstage, holding hands, laughing and breathless, Marigold felt like a runner in a relay race being handed the baton.

"Go, Goldie," whispered Barrie, and she was back onstage for her big scene, searching for the letter. Tears came easily as Lady Sophie coldly dismissed her, and as Polly made her last exit, without the pause, she was rewarded with a round of applause all for herself.

It was over. The curtain call, the thunderous applause and the sense of relief began to shade into a massive feeling of anti-climax. Mrs. Harbour, with two landlady friends, called to the dressing room to give their verdict: "Lovely. We cried, we laughed. Just lovely."

Then a bunch of friends arrived to congratulate Helen, and Marigold felt crushed beyond endurance in the tiny dressing room. As soon as she could, she escaped.

She wandered backstage, where the stage was in darkness. A velvety blackness lapped around her, a blackness that was a soft and friendly cloak for her sense of emptiness.

As she stood there, her eyes closed, she suddenly felt a mouth pressed on hers, a strange, disembodied mouth she could not identify. The kiss was exploratory and gentle, and, driven by curiosity and longing, she could not help responding. A slow, relentless fire in her belly kindled an answering flame in the lips pressed on hers. Their pressure increased, she felt her mouth opening to them, and in the darkness, the dizziness of desire overcame her. But before she could reach out and hold the body that must surely be there, the kiss ended and the mystery presence was gone.

She stumbled back along the corridor, meeting Don, Tina, and Peggy, who were on their way to the restaurant.

"You all right? You look a bit stunned," said Tina.

"Oh, I'm fine, just everything's been a bit...unexpected, I mean overwhelming."

"You were really good, you made me cry," said Tina. "Oh, and did you like the flowers?"

"The marigolds?" She tried to make her voice sound bright. "Yes, thanks, they were from you?"

"Yeah, we've got loads in our garden," said Don.

Oh, thought Marigold, *they live together. They have a garden. That must be nice.*

They made their way to the restaurant—Tina and Peggy were chattering, but Marigold's thoughts were spinning. *That kiss—it surely must have been Tor? Not Barrie, oh please, not him.* She had kissed him back, whoever it was, with a heart and a half, giving herself away in the process. But if it was Tor, why had he not spoken? What was he playing at?

They arrived at the restaurant, where three long tables had been put together. An undignified scramble took place as no one wanted to be on the edges, away from the action. In the center was Tor, of course, with Lydia on one side, wearing an exquisitely cut, skin-tight grey silk dress, and Evelyn on the other. Barrie, with a white carnation in his buttonhole, was next to Evelyn. Marigold was further down the table, with Peggy Grey on one side and a man she did not know on her right.

It should have been fun; there were speeches, and champagne, and jokes, and toasts. The food was delicious, but something was missing.

Marigold tried not to look at Tor, but he was the center of attention, and from the little knot of people around him came the loudest laughter. His glass always seemed to be full—but was it sparkling water or something stronger? And he seemed to have forgotten her existence.

The meal over, the speeches began again. The unknown men in evening dress, who turned out to be business sponsors of the theatre, all had to have their say. Marigold longed for the evening to be over.

Tor was paying attention to everyone who spoke, everyone who caught his eye. She saw Lydia brush her hand along his sleeve and he bent his head to her—whatever it was she whispered to him, it made him smile and nod. Marigold fought back tears, pretending to drop her napkin and blinking madly as she bent to retrieve it.

As she straightened up, Tor looked at her. His eyes were questioning, gentle. She was powerless to look away; her muscles grew weak, and she felt a ton weight pressing on her breast. Then he smiled—a slow, sweet smile intended only for her—and it was as if a firework had exploded in her solar plexus, its starry trail shooting fire along her veins.

Tor raised his glass in a silent toast to her, and drank.

*

The party broke up in the small hours, and Marigold found herself in a taxi with Helen, Evelyn, and Tor. Helen was dropped off first, then Marigold. Tor followed her to the gate of her digs, leaving a sleepy Evelyn nodding in the back of the taxi.

"Marigold. I've been wanting to talk with you all evening."

"You've had plenty of chances to do that," said Marigold, fumbling for her front door key, "but you were too busy with more exciting people."

His hand closed around her wrist like a steel trap. "Listen to me."

She tried unsuccessfully to pull away. "I bloody well won't! You think you can mess about with me and I'll always be there like a puppy waiting for a walk—but I won't!"

"You don't understand—"

"Yes I do, I'm not stupid. You're playing games with me to make Lydia jealous."

"Lydia? Oh, for God's sake—"

"And it was you that kissed me in the dark, wasn't it?"

He let go of her wrist. "Yes, it was. I'm sorry."

"Sorry? I don't understand you! Why can't you be honest with me? What are you hiding?"

Tor stepped back. In the harsh glare of the street light, she saw the play of emotions over his face. That gesture again, the despairing face buried in hands gesture. Was he sincere?

"I can't explain right now. Couldn't you trust me a little?"

Marigold's chin went up and her eyes blazed.

"You're a little too fond of asking women to trust you. Trust has to be earned."

Tor pulled her toward him, and the next moment he was kissing her—not tentatively, but hard and passionately. She felt the rapid beating of his heart against hers, and in spite of herself, she responded to his kiss; fiery and liquid as his mouth was, she wanted more. Suddenly, her hands were tangled in that unruly black hair, pulling his mouth closer and harder against hers, as her heartbeat began to race in the same rhythm as his.

Finally, they stopped to draw breath. Tor was eyeing her with that curious, hard look she could not fathom. Certainly not the expression of a lover.

"Next time I kiss you, there'll be no mistaking me," he said softly, and though the deep cadences of his voice sent a thrill of desire through Marigold's body, she also shook with fury at his arrogance.

"There won't be a next time. I wish I never had to see you again."

It was a great exit line, but he had already turned away.

CHAPTER EIGHT

The days following the first night deepened Marigold's sense of anti-climax, after the press reviews, which were all good, a feeling of weariness set in, leading to niggling moments of pettiness amongst the cast, and occasional discord that left a bad taste in her mouth.

Marigold thought that Lydia, particularly, had taken a special dislike to her—she made Marigold the butt of the occasional waspish comment or raised her wonderful eyebrows at whatever Marigold said. It made her feel so awkward that she actually found herself asking Helen's advice.

"You're right," Helen said. "She's got it in for you. She's not making much headway with Tor, and she thinks you might be in her way."

"But they sat together at the restaurant—she was all over him like a rash that night, and he was grinning as if he liked it."

"Mmm, you are observant, aren't you? But he took you home, not her."

"We only shared a taxi—and Evelyn was there too, so how could anything happen..."

Marigold remembered only too well what had happened that night; since then, she and Tor were barely on speaking terms. But did it matter, as she had hardly seen him since the first night? He had watched the following two performances and given everyone notes, but now his attention was turned to the next production, which they would begin rehearsing in a few days' time.

Tor spent all his time closeted in meetings with Carol Davies and Gavin Merridew, the new designer. Marigold knew that the play was an American murder mystery, with several excellent parts for women, but the idea of starting rehearsals all over again was daunting.

Marigold was looking forward to seeing her parents, and then Betsy, who was coming to see her the following Saturday.

She went to meet her parents at the station on Monday, and seeing their excitement and pleasure, Marigold felt her enthusiasm for the play reviving as they plied her with questions. Her mother had brought a homemade fruitcake and her father a bunch of flowers from the garden at home, as well as a cutting from the local paper describing her as "a young actor of great energy and promise."

The day passed happily as they wandered around the town and listened to news of friends at home. Marigold felt proud as she showed them the theatre, and it was lovely to know they would be out front, watching her with their eyes shining.

Luckily, the show went well and she caught a glimpse of their enthusiastic faces as she took her bows.

Afterwards, they went out for dinner, and her parents were a wonderful audience for her stories about the cast and the experience of being a professional. Her father only looked concerned when she talked endlessly about Barrie, Robin, Brian, and Tor, and finally he asked if she was "going out" with one of them.

"Oh no, Dad!" she protested. "None of them are my type."

"Even though you are playing those very intense love scenes with Barrie?" pursued her mother.

"Good heavens, Ma, it's only a couple of kisses. That's acting," said Marigold glibly. Imagine if her parents had seen her on that dreadful day of rehearsal after her night out with Barrie! It would have confirmed their worst fears.

"Just as long as you don't get yourself into any messy situations…"

Her mother's look to her father, asking for help, provoked more questions from him.

"What about the bad-tempered one?"

"Tor isn't bad-tempered—well, not all the time. He's a brilliant director. But he wouldn't go out with me, I'm just a kid!"

She saw her parents off on the late train, promising that she would keep in touch more conscientiously—unfortunately, they didn't do texting and they weren't on Facebook.

As the train moved out and she waved to them, Marigold was struck by a pang of conscience; she had hardly asked them any questions about the family business or how things were at home.

"I'm beginning to become just the sort of horrible shallow actressy person I would hate to meet myself," she scolded herself as she undressed that night. "Oh, what is wrong with me? Why am I in such a scratchy mood all the time? Why aren't I happy with the luck I have?"

She couldn't wait for Betsy to come and help her sort herself out with some counseling and a bottle of wine.

Before the weekend, however, there was the casting meeting on Wednesday for the new play, *Love is a Poison*.

As the company assembled in the rehearsal rooms that morning, there was a subtle change in the atmosphere from their first meeting. Now they knew each other's strengths and weaknesses, and whereas before all they had wanted was to appear nice and co-operative, now they each had an agenda. Marigold wondered if there might be trouble.

From the moment Tor and Jenny entered the room carrying a stack of scripts, there was tension. Tor stopped Jenny from handing out the scripts immediately.

"Before you see the piece, I'll tell you the story—then you'll see who I've cast," said Tor. He went on to describe the dark, violent thriller about a New York socialite, Amber de Lacey, who is accused of poisoning her lover. Seemingly innocent and charming, she is gradually revealed as sickeningly depraved and dangerously unbalanced. The antagonist, a cynical alcoholic detective, lives in a world of sleazy nightclubs and drug dealers.

The man-eating nightclub singer, Silver Styles, is his only friend. The main characters were supported by a galaxy of minor characters, including Amber's gullible husband and a pathetic woman reporter in love with Harry March, the detective.

Marigold's first thought was that there didn't seem to be a part in there for her at all. Lydia, of course, would play the lead, Amber de Lacey. *Not much acting needed there*, she thought, but she kept a neutral smile on her face as Jenny doled out the scripts.

"Oh, there must be a mistake," said Marigold when she saw the name at the top of her script. "This can't be me, Jenny."

Jenny checked. "Amber de Lacey—yes, that's you."

Marigold felt her heart pounding with excitement. To be given the lead—and what a part! She would really have something to get her teeth into. But then she saw Lydia flash Tor a furious message. He seemed not to have noticed.

"Brian, you get a mixed bag again and this time you get to die twice—once onstage, once off," said Tor, who surely could not have been impervious to the glacial atmosphere emanating from Lydia's corner. "And Helen, you're Patty Doyle, the reporter, and you'll double as Mrs. de Lacey's maid."

Helen nodded, her lips pressed together. Marigold wondered if she had been wanting to be the nightclub singer.

"Lydia, I'd like you to take Silver Styles—"

Lydia rose to her feet. "I am well aware of your likes, Tor," she spat at him with terrifying venom, "and when your professional judgement returns, I may consider a role in this second-rate pot-boiler."

With a gesture of contempt, she flung the script at his feet.

Tor stood up. "Lydia, you will come with me," was all he said as he left the room, not even waiting for her answer.

Eyes flashing, she took in the entire cast with a sneer of loathing, and leapt from the room like a panther.

For a moment they were all frozen, hypnotized by the swing doors, which eerily continued to swing to and fro.

Brian was the first to respond, with a slow handclap. "Oh, bravo, Lydia." He chuckled. "I've never seen a more over the top performance."

"Oh, but what about Tor? Didn't he steal the scene?" Helen suggested, smiling in a satisfied way.

It's all very well for them, thought Marigold. *This doesn't affect them at all. It's me she's angry with—it's me she hates.*

Barrie started patting his pockets, looking for cigarettes. A moment later, he had left the room, seemingly desperate for a smoke. *At least he's keeping his mouth shut,* thought Marigold. *He's quite good-hearted, though he is weak.*

She went over to the big picture windows, wishing she were out in the sunshine. Tor wanted her for the lead! She was stunned, overjoyed. But Lydia wouldn't let it happen. Lydia always got her own way.

Helen, who was leafing through the script, followed her, waving it excitedly. "You've got some cracking scenes—oh, this one's a beauty. You and Lydia have to fight. A real hammer and tongs wrestling match! Have you done any stage fighting?"

"Yes, at drama school."

"And I expect they taught you how to pull punches and cheat the blows so they don't hurt?"

"Of course."

"Well, Lydia learned at quite a different school. She'll be out to draw blood."

"Oh, Helen, leave it! It's not going to happen. I won't be the lead."

Marigold escaped Helen's vicarious delight and found Robin sitting on the stairs outside the rehearsal room, writing furiously.

"What are you doing?"

"Making a shopping list," he said promptly. "I can't bear rows."

So this was a row, thought Marigold. Lydia had finally taken the gloves off. What was Tor thinking, to court her fury? And was she, Marigold, really capable of playing Amber de Lacey? Surely Lydia would do it better?

Ten minutes passed. Brian suggested reading through the script, but no one took him up. Marigold tried to open the script, but her imagination was at work on quite another dialogue—the one happening in Tor's office.

Finally, the swing doors opened and Lydia came in, followed by Tor. Lydia's face was white as marble, her expression impassive. She and Tor sat as far away from each other as possible. He was giving nothing away as he said quietly, "We will now read through."

Lydia said, in a husky whisper, "I'd like to say something. I deeply regret having spoken as I did. It was insulting and inexcusable." Her eyes were fixed on Tor as she spoke, but he did not acknowledge her.

The read through began. The atmosphere of unease and distrust hovering in the air certainly added to the sense of brooding evil in the play; as the reading progressed, they all became gripped with the horror of the story, and Marigold even felt twinges of nausea as the details of Amber de Lacey's descent into evil unfolded.

There was no applause at the end of the play. They all looked at each other as if they had buried something unspeakable.

Tor called a coffee break, and detained Marigold while the others went to the green room. "Are you all right?" he asked casually.

She nodded, fearing that if she spoke, she would burst into tears.

"Good. This part is a big responsibility for you," he said gravely, "and I've given it to you because, if it works, it will be extraordinarily powerful. Your innocence, your freshness will seduce the audience, so your depravity will come as a total shock to them. You won't have any trouble with the innocence, but you are going to have to dig deep down into your psyche to find the dark side of her, and your, personality."

"It is a challenge," said Marigold miserably, thinking how she would have loved this part at drama school, where everyone was so kind and supportive. "But if Lydia—"

Tor gave an exclamation of impatience. "Lydia! It's nothing to do with Lydia! It's about whether you are capable of real, serious acting, not just flitting around with a duster."

Marigold felt insulted at his reference to Polly and wondered if she should hand in her resignation immediately. He was clearly confusing her with someone else, someone who had the brass neck to stand up to a star with a grudge against her.

"I can't play this part if Lydia has decided it should be hers. She'll make life impossible—you know she will."

Tor gave a grimace of distaste. "I obviously overestimated you. I thought you had some backbone under that wide-eyed schoolgirl persona. What happened to the woman who insisted I audition her, even though I'd said no? What happened to the spirit and fire you showed when we went to see Evelyn? Were you only acting then?"

Marigold was speechless. He'd managed to insult her and pay her compliments in the same breath. He thought she was a lightweight, did he? She would show him.

They worked on the play until just after four, since they had a performance that night. Marigold had had time to think up some replies to his earlier comments, and, tired though she was, she could not let him get away with a character assassination. She waited until the others had gone, then called out to him, "I'd like to talk with you, please, Tor."

He nodded. "What about a drink?" he suggested, pleasantly enough. "The Lord Nelson—"

"No, not there—Barrie drinks there."

"Okay, how about Blazers?" Blazers was a wine bar that was one of Lydia's favorite haunts, but Marigold felt ridiculous raising one objection after another.

It was a short walk to Blazers, and Tor was not in a talkative mood. They entered the warm, steamy atmosphere, laden with odors of garlic and wine.

"Want to eat something?" he asked, but Marigold was too wrought up to be hungry. She half-expected Lydia to come in and fly at her with scarlet talons, and the thought of Tor having to separate them in public made her giggle. They found a quiet corner and he ordered coffee. "Okay. Shoot. What is it you want to say?"

His directness was disconcerting. Marigold stirred her coffee, trying to find the right words.

"You—you said I didn't have any backbone. And you were very dismissive about Polly. I just wanted to say I think that was wrong. And unfair."

To her surprise, he didn't argue. "Okay. I apologize. I spoke inappropriately. Anything else?"

"I never know where I am with you—I know you have a lot going on, I'm not being judgmental about your situation—"

"My situation?"

Was he playing with her, laughing at her—or had she hit a nerve? Her heart began thudding; suppose all those things Helen had said were lies? What did she actually know?

"You had to go to London suddenly. And people talked. I don't gossip, but I can't stop other people."

There was a long pause as he looked her in the eye, and she tried not to drop her gaze, feeling that if she did, she would have lost the battle of wills.

"You're quite old-fashioned, aren't you?" he said eventually. "You have a sense of honor that isn't even of this century. It's in the tradition of *Brief Encounter*—you know the film I mean?"

"Of course; I do have an education. And you may laugh at me all you like, but I try to be honest."

He said gently, "It's an engaging quality."

"But this is what I'm getting at. One minute you are being nice, and a few seconds later, you turn into another person altogether."

"A monster, a brute, a beast."

"Don't tease me. I don't know if it's something I said, or other things on your mind, but it's as if you have the script, you know the lines and the moves, and I'm left guessing."

"Well, I am the director..."

"I'm not talking about work! Why did you kiss me in the dark?"

He sighed, dragging his hands through his hair. "Yes, that was taking advantage. But you don't want to know about how complicated my life is. You see everything in black and white, like all nineteen year olds."

"Twenty, I'm twenty. And now you're patronizing me and making excuses!"

"Tell me you didn't want me to kiss you."

He could see into her, he was examining her thoughts, and she could not stare him out.

"Would it have made any difference if I hadn't?"

"Of course."

He put down his cup and said coolly, "Is that it? Have you anything else before I go back to work?"

"Don't! Don't dismiss me like that!"

Marigold had not meant to raise her voice, but in a sudden lull in the conversation in the bar, her words could be clearly heard. Tor stood up and said calmly, "I'm not about to have a scene in public. I'll see you after the show."

He did not wait for her, but flung some money on the table, slung his jacket over his shoulder, and was gone. She sat for a minute, seething with anger, baffled and unsatisfied.

The play went badly that night—the first time the show had lacked pace and sparkle. Marigold was uneasy in her scenes with Lydia, wondering if she might get her own back by some malicious trick onstage. Relieved when the curtain calls were over and nothing dreadful had happened, she ran back to the dressing room, hoping to get changed and away before Tor could find her.

Helen had left, saying that she thought she might have a cold coming and needed an early night. Marigold was about to go when the knock she had been expecting came. A single, decisive knock. It had to be Tor.

Without being asked, he came in, shutting the door behind him. The lazy coolness of his demeanor in the wine bar was gone—in its place was an extraordinary animation and excitement. He seized Marigold's hand, and she felt the rapid pulsing of his energy, firing her with an answering spark.

"Let's go somewhere—anywhere," he said, and started laughing. It was so unexpected that she started laughing too, and they laughed together until they were weak and had to sit down. As they recovered their breath, the door was flung open and Lydia stood on the threshold.

"Carol told me you were here," she said icily.

"As you see, she is correct," he said politely. "How can I be of help?"

"It doesn't matter. It can wait till tomorrow."

And Lydia left.

"I'm sorry. I'll say it as many times as you want to hear it. It's time I was honest with you," Tor said, offering Marigold his palm. She rested her hand in his. "I am in a hideously complicated tangle—but that's no excuse for the way I've been behaving. I can't tell you everything, because I'd be breaking confidences and other people would end up getting hurt. Can I ask you to trust me without provoking a slap in the face?"

He sat, pretending to ward off the blow, and Marigold gave a despairing half laugh, half sob. Why didn't she walk out now, before she got in deeper? Why, when he'd just given her a warning about how he wasn't available, did she have this insane urge to tell him she loved him?

"Come with me." He pulled her to her feet. He was radiating pure excitement, and she felt the electric charge jolting along her veins.

He led her back to the stage area. Everyone else was gone; the lights were dark. The quietness lay on them heavily as velvet.

Marigold heard a match strike, and Tor lit a candle. By its wavering light, they stepped into the eighteenth century drawing room. The heavy red curtains hung between them and the empty auditorium.

Tor put the candlestick on the floor, and turned to face her. In its pale light, the contours of his face were highlighted in gold. He looked at her and nodded, and she went to him—it was she who pulled his mouth down to hers, and she who pressed herself against him.

"Darling girl, what is it? You're shaking..."

Marigold was dizzy with him, with longing, with the wonder of it all.

He took her gently in his arms, stroking her hair and face, and together they lay down on the soft Turkish carpet. This was what she wanted more than anything: Tor's body and mind fiercely concentrated on her, on giving her pleasure. She lay on top of him and, breathing out in a long sigh of anticipation, laid her mouth hotly on his.

The kiss lasted forever.

"I had so many things to tell you," he said as they disentangled and lay side by side, "but right now, none of them matters. What matters is this—do you want me? Do you want me here, now, with no hesitation? Because, my darling, you are everything I want right now."

For answer, she took his hand and kissed the palm, then drew it down to where her heart was pounding. For her, there was no doubt. She wanted to give herself to him, body, heart, mind and soul, and she would do it tonight.

"Wait here," he whispered suddenly. In the dim light of the candle she saw him searching in the wings, then return with his arms full of white draperies.

"Lady Trensham will never know," he said as he laid out the bedding on the floor. The pillows were soft and smelled of lavender soap.

"Now," said Tor.

With shaking fingers, she undid the buttons of his shirt. In the light of the candle, his skin was gold and bronze. She wriggled out of her clothes, and soon they were naked, devouring each other with their eyes, kissing, touching, whispering.

His hand rested lightly, tantalizingly on her breast. Drawing his fingers up the nipple, he teased it into hardness, then, bending his head, his tongue curled around its stiffness with a maddening pleasure that overwhelmed her with an ache of longing. But he was in no hurry—he suckled gently, then fiercely; the hotness of his mouth plucked a quivering response from her, as if he had drawn a bow across the invisible cello string that ran from breast to belly. Slowly, unbearably slowly, he traced the line of that quivering string, stroking along her belly until his fingers reached the place where pleasure begins. She began to move her body against his hand, responding to mounting intensity with instinctive, urgent thrusts. At last, with a low moan of pleasure, she abandoned herself to the waves of sweetness that engulfed her, flooding her, discovering her, leaving her breathless and trembling.

Tor was all softness now—joyful, intimate, and vulnerable. He stroked the damp hair back from her face and she opened herself to him. As his lips traced the line of her neck and throat, she reached down to touch him, to hold him, to press that hot hardness against her fingers as she had pressed against his.

"Are you sure?" was all he said. But she opened herself to him and, pulling him on top of her, guided him into her. It was done in a moment, and the pain, if there was any, was of a piercing sweetness that made her cry out and cling to him, drawing him in deeper. For a second he was still, fixing her with burning eyes, and she felt herself take fire from their dark flame. Then he began to move, and as she felt him searching and probing her innermost secrets, that sweet pain began again and they were both moving, faster, harder, hotter, until, with a long shuddering breath, Tor gave himself to her. In the same heartbeat, the aching waves of pleasure lifted her higher and higher until, when she could bear it no more, the intensity of her release found its voice in a long, sobbing, wordless cry.

They lay, too exhausted to move, their limbs tangled together. Marigold felt Tor's heart slowing against her breast. His breathing calmed to slower pace. Cradling his face in her hands, she was astonished to see tears in his eyes.

"Tor, darling, what's wrong?"

Fiercely, he shook the tears away. "Oh, why can't it always be like this? So new and—so perfect?" He drew away from her. "I'm crushing you to death."

He lay on his back and she snuggled into his embrace. In the quiet darkness that lapped them both, she laid her head on his shoulder and fell into the sweetest of sleeps.

*

Marigold jumped awake, not knowing how long she had slept. Hours or days, it didn't matter to her. The space beside her was empty, and, the candle having burnt down, she was in darkness. She stretched and lay down again.

There was no going back. She had given herself to Tor with no commitment, no declaration of love. His lovemaking had been wonderfully tender and gentle—but what did that prove?

There was a lamp in the prompt corner that suddenly came alive, sending delicate shafts of slanting light across the stage. Tor appeared, with a sheet knotted round his waist. He was carrying a tray of tea things, which he laid beside her.

"You're still here," he said, pouring her fragrant tea into Lady Sophie's favorite cup.

"I couldn't leave—I couldn't find my clothes in the dark."

"Good," he said, grinning.

They drank their tea.

"Isn't it your birthday on Friday?" he said suddenly.

"How do you know that?"

"It's on your C.V. How are you planning to celebrate your twenty-first?"

"I can't think of any better rite of passage this," said Marigold.

"Your first time?"

She felt herself blushing as she nodded.

"I am honored." Tor bent his head, kissing her fingertips. "Come away with me."

"How? When?"

"After the show on Friday. We'll drive to a little village down the coast, we'll have a night away together—" But suddenly Tor broke off. "Damn."

"What's wrong?"

He stood up and began to dress. "Nothing. Nothing important. Let's do it. Will you come away with me? Say you will. I'll put everything else on hold." He stroked his fingers down her bare arm. "*You* are important."

"How could I say no? It would be lovely."

He kissed her cheek. "You're freezing—come on, get some clothes on."

"Where are we going?"

"Home to our beds. I'm taking you back to your digs and I shall return to the Sovereign. We both need a decent night's sleep."

Marigold, in a delicious dream state, dressed herself while Tor tidied everything away, leaving no trace of their presence.

As they left the theatre, Tor put his arm around her, and she leaned into the confident, strong curves of his body, feeling that she had come home at last.

CHAPTER NINE

Marigold had assumed that she and Tor would have time to talk during a break in rehearsals the next day, but there was a radio interview for the BBC that took him, Lydia, and Barrie away during the lunch break. It was an odd sensation, going through the mechanics of rehearsal, pretending that nothing had happened. She could not help sneaking sidelong glances at that expressive face, remembering it softened in the candlelight by their lovemaking. Surely he must be thinking of her in the same way? But he gave no sign of it, as, frowning with concentration, he guided the cast around the tape marks of the new set.

After lunch, they had reached scene five. Amber de Lacey and the singer, Silver Styles, were the only characters in this scene—and it was where they had to have the no-holds-barred physical fight. Marigold was beginning to feel nervous already—but Tor turned a few pages of his script, saying casually, "Let's pick up from scene six."

Lydia gave an exclamation of surprise, and he nodded to her and Marigold.

"I can let everyone else go after the tea break, and we three can tackle the fight then, if that suits you?" The question was a formality. They would, of course, do as he said.

Marigold took up her position for scene six. Lydia was smiling, a tiny, secret smile of anticipation that sent alarm bells ringing in Marigold's head. What mischief was she planning?

All I need to do is be completely professional about scene five, she told herself. The tea break over, the rest of the cast gathered up their things and left, happy to be given a few hours of unexpected freedom. Jenny Warren was in town buying props. Marigold wished she had been with them. There was a horrible intimacy about the three of them alone together.

Lydia was leaning against the long window that looked out onto the sea, her arms folded and her clouds of black hair silhouetted in the afternoon light. She turned and faced into the room, her eyes following Tor, lashes fluttering like the wings of a moth around its fatal candle. She was poised, tensed to strike, only waiting for her prey; something very like terror began to crawl along Marigold's spine.

Tor had put two chairs and a table on the space marked for the stage, and he stood reading the script, one hand in his pocket, seemingly oblivious to the atmosphere of unease in the room.

"I haven't plotted this at all—we'll wing it," he announced. Marigold wondered why. Usually, Tor had all the moves blocked meticulously. Could it be that he was nervous too? He was certainly not giving any sign of it.

Lydia, with a snake-like, rippling gesture, pulled off the loose blouse she was wearing. Underneath was a skin-tight crimson suntop with spaghetti straps. Marigold could not help but notice how tall she was, how elegant, how long her legs and how creamy-ivory her arms and shoulders were. Impatiently Lydia shook off the high-heeled sandals she was wearing and stretched, like a tiger waking from sleep.

"You'd better remove those earrings, too," said Tor, in a relaxed, even humorous tone, as if he knew perfectly well what Lydia was up to. Lydia took off the gold hoops and threw them playfully to Tor. He caught them, of course.

"Marigold—any clothes you would like to discard and throw my way?"

He was enjoying this, she thought. She wished his enjoyment was contagious, but it only made her feel more apprehensive. She took off her shoes, hating her smallness next to the goddess-like Lydia.

"Okay, to work. Let's have Silver here—" he lightly pulled the willing Lydia into position "—and Amber facing her, here." Marigold let herself be positioned opposite her rival.

Tor asked them to put down their scripts, which made her feel even more naked.

He directed in a hands-on, flowing way, moving them about, standing very close. At one stage, he stood behind Lydia, drawing her arm back to demonstrate a blow, and with a jolt Marigold remembered how he had done the same when he taught her to skim stones on the beach.

"Now Amber takes hold of Silver's left arm and bends it behind her back, like this." Tor demonstrated, twisting Lydia into a kneeling position. Marigold could not bear to see the pleasure it gave Lydia to be manhandled by him.

"Good. Now, Silver, pull Amber down on the ground and sit astride her—yes, that's it, excellent—and demonstrate your power, do something to make her feel she's lost the battle—"

Without a pause, Lydia raked her long fingernails down the side of Marigold's cheek. *Ouch! That hurt, that really stung*, Marigold thought. Struggling to throw the weight of the taller woman off her, Marigold expected to see a look of shock or remorse in her eyes as she felt the blood trickle down her cheek. But all she could see was a ruthless, implacable hatred. Slowly, Lydia increased the pressure on Marigold's upper arm, leaning on it with her bony knee, grinding the bicep painfully into the bone. The fight had turned real. Marigold shoved her free hand under her opponent's ribs and tickled her as roughly as she could. Lydia relaxed her grip, surprised, and Marigold twisted her bent leg up into Lydia's chest and pushed with all her strength.

Lydia went flying backwards. Marigold leapt to her feet, ready for a sneak attack. But Lydia was lying on her back, breathing loudly and dramatically, eyes closed, not moving.

"Oh my God, you've killed her," said Tor—but he sounded as if he was going to burst out laughing.

"Have I knocked her out?"

Marigold knelt by the motionless figure, and gently replaced one of the straps which had slid from Lydia's shoulder during the fight, revealing the top of one creamy breast.

Tor's lips twitched with amusement. He knelt beside Marigold, lifting Lydia's head onto his lap. Her eyelids began to flutter.

"Marigold, be an angel and get some water," he said.

In the mirror in the bathroom, she had time to inspect her own wound—it was the merest scratch, but it smarted.

Returning with the glass of water, she saw that Tor was delicately feeling the back of Lydia's head—his hands were buried deep in those raven tresses, massaging softly. Lydia was giving little sighs of either pain or pleasure.

Marigold toyed with the idea of throwing the water over them both, but Tor quickly took the glass and encouraged Lydia to sit up and take some dainty sips. The floor was soft vinyl—they all knew she could not really have hurt herself. *Anyway,* thought Marigold, *it was entirely her own fault.*

"All right now?" asked Tor, with just the right blend of solicitousness and briskness.

Lydia instantly stopped playing the part of wounded victim, and became instead the gallant heroine. "It hurt like hell. But let's get on with the show."

"How about you, Marigold?" asked Tor, looking at the scratch on her face with a raised eyebrow.

"I'm fine."

Tor left Lydia and took Marigold's face in his hands to examine the wound, and immediately Lydia sprang up and came over, replacing Tor's hands with her own.

"Oh, you poor child. I don't know my own strength. I only intended to cheat that; you must have moved, I am abjectly sorry."

"I'll be ready for you next time," said Marigold, trying to keep her voice neutral.

"Splendid. Then let's pick up from where we stopped. I'll give you rather more exact direction, so we can avoid further injuries, hopefully," said Tor.

The spectacle of two women fighting for his attention may have given him some amusement, but Marigold knew that this was just an opening salvo in an undeclared war between herself and a more experienced, malicious opponent.

They worked on the fight until it was perfect. All three knew it would be a show-stopper. It was hard physically, but it also depended on exact timing and cooperation between the two actors. Marigold felt by the end of the day that Lydia had some respect at least for her junior's stage fighting ability, and would not be trying any more dirty tricks in scene five.

Which still left Lydia a lot of opportunities in other areas.

"The casting works well," said Tor at the end of the rehearsal. "And you've done a good afternoon's work. You can have a late call tomorrow—eleven o'clock. Now go home and get some rest."

He disappeared back to his office. Lydia and Marigold eyed each other warily. Lydia lit a cigarette.

"You're a little girl with spirit," said Lydia, blowing smoke toward her.

"Put that out. There's no smoking in here, you know very well."

Lydia raised her eyebrows. "What are rules for but to be broken?" Lydia picked up her bag. "I think you'll find he prefers naughty girls to good girls. Or maybe he's corrupted you already?"

"You know nothing," said Marigold, feeling anger rising in her throat.

"Oh, I know Tor very well indeed. We're old and very close friends, Tor and I."

Lydia stubbed out her cigarette and put on her shoes. She shook her hair back from her face and Marigold felt the musky cloud of her sensual perfume insinuating itself into her nostrils.

"The attractive thing about him is that he always gets what he wants."

"And what about you, Lydia? Do you always get what you want?"

The mocking smile disappeared from Lydia's face and she became a mask of steely determination. "Oh yes. Always."

Her voice was deep and thrilling, and the naked ambition it exposed sent a shiver along Marigold's spine. But she wasn't going to be bullied.

"Same time tomorrow, then, sister," she said, as lightly as she could, leaving the room before Lydia had time to think of a crushing answer.

*

It was Friday. Marigold was deeply asleep when Mrs. Harbour knocked at her door and brought in a satisfyingly large bundle of cards and a cup of tea. It was her birthday!

"Special treatment for you today, my lady," said Mrs. Harbour, who knew everything. She sang, "She's got the key of the door, never been twenty-one before!"

"Thank you. And...could I ask you a favor? May I use your kitchen to make a cake? I'd like to have something to share with everyone tonight."

Mrs. Harbour's round face beamed with pleasure. "Bless you, you won't have time to make a cake—you've got rehearsals today. Why don't I do it? I'm world famous for my cakes. I can have it ready for when you come back at teatime. What flavor, and how big do you want it?"

There was no card from Tor. Everyone else had remembered—her parents, her friends from home and from London, her aunts and uncles. There was one small package, with a local postmark. Maybe Tor had sent her a present!

It was from Barrie. Some expensive and cloyingly over-perfumed soap, and a card signed "Adoringly yours." But she didn't want cards and presents from Barrie.

He was the first person she saw when she arrived for rehearsal, leaning against the outside wall of the Tower Theatre in a pose straight from his TV role, smoking. As soon as he saw her, he tossed the cigarette away.

"Happy Birthday, golden Goldie!" he sang out, more or less claiming a hug and kiss. Lydia arrived as they drew apart, giving her a quizzical look and knowing smirk that remained on her face, even after Marigold's hasty explanation that it was her birthday.

Tor was sitting at the director's table, talking to Jenny. He broke off to welcome everyone, but said nothing special to Marigold, nothing celebratory. Maybe he had forgotten. Marigold put on the high heels she was rehearsing in as Amber de Lacey, biting her tongue to stop the tears that threatened. Then Barrie entered, shouting, "It's our Goldie's birthday today!" which lead to a round of wishes and hugs that made Marigold feel embarrassed. Weren't birthdays a childish excuse for attention?

Tor, standing up to begin the day's work, caught her eye and said, "Happy Birthday. I hope it's everything you wished for."

Had he forgotten they were going away together tonight? Were his eyes telegraphing a secret message? Marigold looked away. She would not give him the satisfaction of gazing at him hungrily. She was going to concentrate on her work today.

Love is a Poison was taking shape more quickly than the first play; the company was more into the rhythm of working together, and their minds were focused. There was a sense of excitement in the air as Lydia and Marigold took up their positions for scene five.

The fight went well. Marigold had no idea what the rest of the cast thought about it—until the table sequence. She and Lydia grappled together and pulled each other onto the table, then after a sequence of acrobatic wrestling rolled onto the floor. The other actors reacted with gasps of surprise, whistles, and a startled cry from Jenny. As the fight ended, Barrie led everyone in a round of applause, in which Tor joined.

"Well done," was all he said quietly, but it meant more to Marigold than any superlatives. Maybe he had forgotten her birthday, but he still knew how to give her the best gift of all—his passionate attention.

They all went to the café together, and Marigold was treated to her lunch. Never had an avocado and prawn baguette tasted so good. Tor sat next to her; as the lunch hour ended, everyone else melted away, leaving them alone.

"You thought I'd forgotten?" he teased. "After what I said to you on Wednesday night?" He reached into his pocket and brought out a small—a very small—box. It had the name of a well-known Branchester jeweler on it.

"I didn't want to give you this in front of everyone," he said.

She opened it, her heart thudding.

Inside was a delicate gold chain with a small flower pendant.

"They told me it was a daisy, but to me, it looked exactly like a marigold," he said. "Happy birthday, darling."

He kissed her, and even in that crowded café, she felt her senses drowning in a delicious, dizzy ache of longing. She kissed him back, wishing they were alone and naked. He stroked his hand down her back and murmured softly in her ear, "We'll celebrate properly tonight."

"Thank you. It's lovely. Are we really going away together?"

"Mm—I have to make a couple of phone calls, but I don't think there'll be a problem. I'll hire a car, and we can disappear off the face of the earth for a while."

Marigold floated back to rehearsal, feeling that she was capable of anything. She enjoyed getting her teeth into her new character, the deceptively well-bred and soft-spoken Mrs. de Lacey—and

Tor knew exactly when to keep quiet and let her find her own way, and when to come up with a simple yet dazzling idea that enhanced his vision of the piece, and helped her, as an actor, to achieve her goals.

Of course, he had been right about the other play, too, asking her to cut the pause—but Marigold still wondered if he had been put under pressure to do that from Lydia.

The tea break was just coming to an end, and Barrie was giving out a general invitation to everyone for Saturday night, when there was going to be a big party at one of the most luxurious houses in town, when Carol Davies came in, looking flustered.

"Tor, dreadfully sorry to bother you in rehearsal, but it's urgent," she said. He went outside the rehearsal room and they could see them having a whispered conversation. Too far away to hear what was being said, Marigold could only watch through the window of the swing door.

"Goldie, you'll come, won't you?" urged Barrie. "It's going to be massive. Mike and Marla are huge sponsors of the Tower. There'll be a band, loads of interesting people, and fabulous food. Have I convinced you?"

Marigold wondered if she and Tor would be able to get any time together over the weekend. But maybe that wouldn't matter, if they spent her birthday night together.

"My friend Betsy will be here—can I bring her?"

"If she's as gorgeous as you, no problem. I'll give you both a lift, it's a few miles out of town."

Carol and Tor had disappeared. Marigold tried not to think what was going on.

Evelyn and Brian approached her next with an offer to take her out for a birthday dinner—a proposal which Marigold smilingly refused.

But Evelyn was gently persuasive. "You wouldn't say no to a quick drink in the bar after the show?"

Evelyn rarely socialized, so Marigold felt it was only polite to say yes. Surely Tor wouldn't mind leaving half an hour later? "That would be lovely."

Suddenly, everyone was coming for drinks—even Lydia. "We can't let a twenty-first go uncelebrated, can we?" she said, as Marigold wondered if this was such a good idea.

Ten minutes passed. Then fifteen, and Tor had not returned. When the swing doors opened, it was Carol who came in.

"Message from Tor," she announced. "He's tied up with a phone call and it could take half an hour. Jenny, could you run the second act? Then everyone is free to go."

After Carol left, there was a buzz of gloomy speculation.

"Tor should sort out his private life in his own time," said Lydia.

"How can you be so sure it's private?" challenged Marigold.

Lydia shrugged. "If it isn't, then this looks rather like professional incompetence. Not what our esteemed director would wish anyone to think, surely?"

"What business call would take half an hour?" Helen chipped in.

Barrie broke the tension by saying, "My agent, renegotiating my contract."

There was laughter, but Marigold could not join in. Something was wrong. Something was going to come between her and that wonderful romantic escape Tor had promised.

*

Mrs. Harbour came up trumps with a beautiful cake, with Marigold's name iced on it. "No candles, though," she said. "They only get in the way when you're trying to cut it."

Before that night's show, Marigold called to all the dressing rooms and shared her cake with the actors. Tina and Peggy got slices too; they were beavering away at the thirties' costumes for the new play. And Don got a chunk to divide with his crew.

The only person she could not find was Tor. Jenny said he was "somewhere around," but when she tried his office, it was locked.

It was impossible for Marigold to enter into the spirit of the play that night. She struggled to concentrate, but her mind constantly came up with images of Tor—having a row with an ex-wife on the phone, driving furiously to some secret destination, or simply alone, staring out to sea as he had the night of the dress rehearsal, with that unfathomable, despairing expression on his face.

As soon as the curtain was down and she was changed out of her costume, Marigold hurried to the circle bar. Brian greeted her with a flourish—he'd gotten a bunch of flowers for her, and there was a card everyone had signed. Soon they were sitting down with drinks.

"You've been a bit of an angel to Evelyn, she tells me," he said softly, toasting her. "She is such a wonderful lady, but so easily upset. Ever since you sprung her out of that ghastly place she was in—"

"Oh, that wasn't me, that was Tor. He moved her to the Sovereign."

"She responded to a woman's kindness," he repeated firmly.

Barrie and Robin joined them, and soon the drinks were flowing. No matter how quickly Marigold emptied her glass, there always seemed to be another full one in front of her.

"Brian says you have a secret assignation," said Barrie, as she began to wonder if everyone else was keeping up with her intake.

"No secret. I'm going out with a friend. I have made some friends here, you know," she said cheekily.

Luckily, Jenny arrived to cut short any further cross-examination. Everyone wanted to know where Tor was.

"I'm really sorry, I don't know," she admitted. "I had things to do in town after the rehearsal. I thought he would be here."

Marigold took another gulp of wine. That was it, then. He'd run out on her. Unsteadily, she got to her feet and went to the box office, hoping to find Carol. She was there as usual, checking the receipts with the front of house manager.

"Carol, I really need to know this. Is Tor in the building?"

Carol looked up from her work, frowning. Her words were careful. "He had to go to a meeting this afternoon."

"What kind of meeting? Where?"

Marigold knew her voice was too loud, but at least she wasn't swaying about like a stage drunk.

Carol was staring at her now—was that look critical or sympathetic? "I'm sure he'll make up for lost rehearsal time—"

"It's not that. Can I tell you this in confidence? He promised to take me out tonight. Because it's my birthday. He promised."

"I'm sorry," Carol said eventually, "he's not here. He had to go to London."

"London? Then—he won't be back tonight?"

Carol must have heard how her voice wobbled. She gave Marigold a tissue before she answered. "If he could, he would have let people know—"

"People! I'm not people! And I suppose this is nothing to do with work. It's personal. Isn't it?"

Carol did not need to answer. Her face told Marigold she was right.

"Thank you," Marigold said, with as much lofty dignity as she could muster. "You've been very helpful."

She went back to the bar in a reckless mood. Evelyn offered to buy her a brandy cocktail—what the hell? She'd never had a cocktail. She tried it, and it was delicious, so Helen bought her another.

Time seemed to pass rather swiftly after that.

Then Barrie was sitting next to her with his arm round her, saying, "My God, that fight between you and Lydia is going to steal the show—I was gobsmacked."

"That's nothing." Marigold giggled. "Lydia actually drew blood—didn't you, Lydia?"

There was no Lydia.

"Has anyone seen Lydia?" said Marigold, feeling stupid.

Evelyn, who shared a dressing room with her, said, "She's in London, I believe. Something came up unexpectedly."

Yes, thought Marigold to herself, *I'll bet it did*. Something tall and dark and handsome who she'd had her hooks into for weeks—if not years. Lydia had gotten Tor. She was in London with him now. She was probably in bed with him.

Marigold detached herself from Barrie, who was stroking her hair and murmuring some soft invitation. She had to get out of this bar. She had to be on her own. She needed some fresh air.

She stumbled outside, feeling the cold east wind as it hit her like a blow in the face. How many drinks had she had? She realized that she hadn't eaten since lunchtime—so why was she feeling so sick? She leaned against the wall, groaning.

The stage door opened and Tina and Don came out.

"Ooh, someone's been celebrating," said Tina, but Don took her arm and said, "Are you okay?"

"He stood me up. I don't care. I feel a bit..."

"Okay, this is what we're going to do," said Don, as Marigold started crying. "You're coming home with us and we're going to intravenously give you coffee until you feel better."

"Oh, what a thing to do on your birthday!" exclaimed Tina. "One of these days, Barrie's going to get a taste of his own medicine."

"Not Barrie!" Marigold dissolved in a fresh burst of tears. "I don't care about Barrie."

"Don't say anything until we get behind closed doors," said Don kindly, helping her into his 2CV.

Tina sat in the back with her arm round Marigold, who hoped she would never feel as bad as this ever again.

"We'll have some tea, and then Don will run you back to your digs, and tomorrow you'll have forgotten all about this," said Tina.

"I'll never forget...feel so humiliated..." Marigold knew she was making an idiot of herself—but it was all Tor's fault! She should be with him!

Tina's house was in a little Victorian terrace in a quiet street far away from the coast. She'd decorated it with stencils in glowing, jewel-like colours. Small lamps cast warm shadows on the stripped pine floorboards. There were big soft cushions on the floor, and antique rugs.

Marigold wished she weren't living in digs.

Don made them all some tea, and Tina lit a fire in the little cast iron fireplace.

It was a proper home. Marigold sat on the small squashy sofa, hoping she had not made a complete fool of herself.

"Ah, don't worry—we've all been there," said Tina.

"Those shelves are crooked, I told you they were," said Don, eyeing them critically. "I'll redo them at the weekend."

"Don't you dare, Don Burlington! They may be crooked, but they are all my own work. You can get on with the kitchen cupboards if you want to make some improvements."

Don made a face at Tina, then blew her a kiss. "More tea, anyone? How are you doing, Marigold?"

"I'm feeling better. You rescued me from a nightmare."

"Want to talk about it?" asked Tina.

Marigold hesitated, but only for a moment. She suddenly felt very lonely. "I was supposed to be going away with Tor tonight. He asked me. He doesn't want the others to know, but we...I thought we were an item. He and I...oh, well, you know, it's the oldest story in the book. I was naïve, and I fell for him. Any recipes for falling out of love with a bastard?"

Tina said quietly, "Tor's not like that. He's preoccupied, and he can be a bit abrupt sometimes. But—"

"He's gone to London! Carol Davies told me. And Evelyn told me Lydia had gone too. I'm not stupid. I can add up two and two."

"Even if you make it five?" said Don. "That's not my experience of Tor. He's straight, and he never tells a lie. Not like some in this business."

"But Lydia's out to get him. She told me so. And how can any man not be attracted to her when she's made her mind up?"

"Because he'd be mad," said Tina. "She's dynamite. She's wonderful onstage, and she looks amazing in her frocks, but she's obsessed with herself and she has no time to be nice to me and Peggy. She calls us 'the little people.' She's bawled us out more than once."

"Which I can vouch for," said Don.

"Okay, but what about the other mistakes he's made? He seems to have made some bad choices before. Apparently, he's had three wives."

"Well," said Tina emphatically, "I don't know anything about that, but I do know that if you are successful in this business you'll have a lot of envious people sniping away at you behind your back. It's all gossip."

"Tina's right," added Don. "Try and rise above it."

Tina gave Marigold a hug. "You look much better. It's not much for a birthday dinner, but would you like to have some cauliflower cheese with us?"

After her tears were over, Marigold loved the peace and quiet of that evening with Don and Tina. They told her they'd only recently started living together, and were obviously still at the stage of mutual discovery that lends magic to the most mundane conversations. *They make a good couple,* thought Marigold. *They will be true to each other, and I think I can trust them; they won't be telling tales about me at the theatre. Imagine the trouble I'd have been in now if I'd gone back to Barrie's place!*

Don dropped her home just after midnight, and she crawled thankfully into bed.

She was drifting off to sleep when she thought she heard the distant ringing of the phone and Mrs. Harbour shuffling along the corridor and picking it up. Her voice sounded surprised, then she protested, and the next minute, she was tapping at Marigold's door.

"Miss Aubrey? You awake?"

Marigold opened the door, blinking.

"He says it's urgent. I told him this is not to become a habit, and I hope you will make that clear to him, whoever he is." Mrs Harbour went back to her room, deeply offended.

"Hello?"

"Marigold?" It was Tor.

"Do you know what time it is? What do you want?" She put all the contempt she could into her answering whisper.

There was a long silence. Marigold was tempted to slam down the phone. He could keep his explanations and apologies.

When he spoke, his voice was passionate. "I love you. That's all."

Then he put the phone down.

CHAPTER TEN

Betsy's train was late, and the station was thronged with holidaymakers as Marigold waited by the barrier, wondering how long it would be before Betsy guessed that something important was up with her friend. Marigold didn't want the whole world to know what was going on until she knew herself. But Betsy had a genius for sniffing out romantic problems. She would know just by looking at her that something was going on.

Distraction was the order of the day, thought Marigold. The play and the party and lots of exciting people to meet. Then, if she needed a shoulder to cry on, Betsy would be there, after herself and Tor had had whatever conversation they needed to. Or rather, *she* needed. Tor seemed to have another agenda all his own.

Betsy flung her arms around Marigold; she was in a high state of excitement already.

"Lydia Dawlish was on the train, in first class, with loads of hangers-on and reporters. They monopolized the bar all the way from London."

They were coming along the platform now, a noisy, self-absorbed bunch of London people, and in the middle, like a black widow spider in her web, was Lydia. She was radiant and laughing and her arm was linked with a man's—but that man was not Tor. A silver-haired American with a swaggering walk and a loud voice was getting all her attention as he swept her out of the station and into a taxi.

"Wow," said Betsy.

"Wow is not the word I would use," said Marigold coldly.

"But you have to admit, she is a star."

"Oh, definitely. But stars can be a total pain in the arse."

"Wow," said Betsy again. "You've certainly changed your tune. So she's not your best friend, then?"

"Look, let's not talk about her. I want to know about you, about the auditions you've done, and your new photos, and what plays you've seen in London?"

Marigold sighed with relief as Betsy's conversation was diverted until they were safely out of the station.

"What would you like to do first?" she asked after they had dumped Betsy's bag at Mrs. Harbour's. "We could have some lunch?"

"No thanks, I had a pork pie and some coffee on the train. Let's go to your theatre. I want to see the posters and your dressing room and everything."

Marigold agreed reluctantly, hoping she would not run into Tor. She wasn't ready. But there was no chance of creeping round the theatre surreptitiously with her exuberant friend in tow. Betsy demanded to be introduced to everyone they met, and before long Marigold had told her about the party Barrie was taking them to that night.

"*Barrie Leicester* is giving you and me a lift?" Betsy kept saying, her voice a squeal of delight. Marigold decided not to tell her about the nightmare date she had had with Barrie—why spoil her friend's pleasure? Betsy was looking fantastic—she'd spent a lot of time at the gym, she'd been on a wholefood diet, and she'd done something new with her eyes, which were dark and smoldering. *Yes*, thought Marigold, *Betsy will make quite an impression tonight.*

They were in her dressing room giggling and chattering, and Betsy was trying on Polly's costume, pulling silly faces and doing comic curtseys. Marigold was beginning to feel relaxed and safe—Tor would hardly come looking for her there. And it was fun, absolutely, to have her friend being so admiring and enthusiastic about everything. Marigold knew how lucky she was.

Suddenly, there was a knock at the door.

"Polly—you're fired," said a stern voice.

Her heart jumped into her mouth—but it was only Barrie. His eyes were twinkling as he took in the scene and joined them, quite sure of his welcome.

"Are you two sisters, or what?" he asked. "Marigold, where have you been hiding this glorious creature?"

"We're very old friends. We were at drama school together."

"Ah, so you're the one who's going to be my guest of honor at the party tonight?"

Barrie reached out for a handshake, giving Betsy the full benefit of his long-lashed blue eyes and his most devastating smile. "I'm Barrie Leicester."

"Pleased to meet you. Elizabeth Oliver," said Betsy in such a low-key, casual way that Marigold wondered if she had taken a sudden dislike to her former heartthrob.

"Great, see you later." And Barrie wandered off.

Betsy waited until he was well out of earshot before she said anything. "I'm going to faint! He's gorgeous! He's exactly like Eddie, but even more sexy in the flesh! How on earth do you keep your hands off him?"

"I don't," said Marigold, laughing. "I get two snogs off him a day—and four on matinee days. Which reminds me, it's time to get ready. Go and get your comp—it's at the box office."

The matinee audience was loud and appreciative that day. Lydia's clique made their presence felt by loud applause, whistles, and whoops at the end of each scene. The final curtain call received a standing ovation, in which Betsy enthusiastically joined.

Marigold enjoyed it all. It was over the top, of course, but it was huge fun to have your efforts so rewarded. And she was delighted the show had gone so well with Betsy out front.

She was in the dressing room before Marigold and Helen had their makeup off, loudly praising them both and asking all the right questions about the technical side of the production. They were all a little giddy when a brisk knock at the door stopped them all in mid-sentence.

Oh no, thought Marigold. *Not Tor, not now.*

"Come in!" called Helen merrily.

It was Barrie.

"Now, girls, after that triumph, I think we all deserve a little drink, don't you?"

"Green room for me," said Helen. "If they are like that at the matinee, who knows what they'll be like this evening? I need a rest."

Marigold had no chance to refuse; Betsy's eyes were fixed pleadingly on hers.

"A quick one," she said.

"Okay. Blazers for a sandwich?" And Barrie led the way.

He was conducting a major charm offensive on Betsy, and Marigold found it funny, watching her friend falling for the Leicester chat-up line while she pretended to be super-cool.

Marigold could not resist asking him, "Will Jenny be there tonight?" For everyone in the company knew that, failing more exciting company, Jenny was always willing to be Barrie's companion.

"Not sure. Poor love, she thinks she's coming down with a cold."

By the time they had got back to the theatre, Barrie had his arm casually around Betsy, and as she went over the finer points of his performance, he was all admiration of her powers of observation.

"You're not really going to sit through it all again? Won't it bore the pants off you?" he asked her.

"Wouldn't miss it for the world," said Betsy, blowing him a kiss as she disappeared into the foyer.

It was getting dark now. Tor must surely be back from London.

Marigold asked Teddy, the dozy old stage door keeper, if he'd seen him.

"No, and you know me, Eagle Eyes. He's not been in today. There's his post."

*

By the time the evening performance was over, Marigold's reservations about meeting Tor had given way to an overpowering desire to see him again.

At intervals during the day, that telephone conversation had played over and over in her head. She had questions to ask him. She wanted to hear him say those words again, looking her in the eye. She wanted a great many things, and only he could provide them.

Her reluctance to leave the theatre was noticed by Betsy as they crossed the road to the market square, where Barrie had told them to meet. The streets were busy: people spilled out of the pubs and cafes, and there was live music playing. There was some excitement in the air, and Marigold wondered if she was going to be part of it. How would this evening end?

Soon they were in Barrie's car, zipping along the road, leaving the bright lights behind them, as Barrie took the coast road, which climbed up from Branchester to the north.

About a mile out of town, he turned into a drive bordered with glossy rhododendrons. Ahead, they could see the pale outline of a large house. As they pulled up, they could hardly find a space among the expensive cars already parked outside, and by the headlights of Barrie's car, Marigold saw the façade of a white Georgian house with a wide sweep of stone steps up to the front door, flanked with pillars. Lights were blazing from every window, and the insistent bass rhythms of the band seemed to enter Marigold's bloodstream, setting her pulses throbbing with its insistent beat. The night air was heavy with the scent of tiny purple and pink flowers—some night-scented stock that grew all along the drive. On the first floor, a large balcony gave onto the sea; there were already couples up there, gazing dreamily at the moon's reflection, which created a path of silver away to the horizon, over the quiet waters.

Betsy caught Marigold's eye, and mouthed a silent "Wow!" which Marigold this time could only repeat back to her. It was ludicrously over the top, but at the same time fabulous that they should be part of this fantasy.

The front door was open, and Barrie stood back to let them in, to be met by a short tubby man in a dinner jacket.

"Barrie!" he cried. "Not a minute too soon—they're all clamoring for you."

"As if," said Barrie.

"Introduce me to your delightful—er—sisters?"

"Mike, meet Betsy and Marigold. Two very talented young actors you will hear more of," said Barrie. "And this is our generous host, Mike Russell, and somewhere in there is his better half."

"Ah yes, the lady of the house—go find her. Music's that way, food that way—you know your way around, Barrie. Mi casa es tu casa."

He disappeared behind a throng of people.

"Well, darlings, what's your pleasure?" asked Barrie—but his question was addressed to Betsy.

"Let's dance!"

Betsy grabbed Marigold's hand as Barrie steered her toward the music, and Marigold was glad; violent physical activity seemed to suit her mood just then. The volume of the music drowned out any attempt at conversation—they all became part of a massive music machine, throbbing and booming. In the thick press of the crowd, Marigold soon got separated from the other two, but she didn't care. She was fed up with taking responsibility for others. She danced until she was exhausted.

Finally the band took a break, and she wandered off to find something to eat and drink.

The food was stunning, and there was plenty of it, and no end of charming young waiters wandering around with glasses of wine. Marigold refused all of them and stuck to orange juice. Brian and Evelyn were tucking into the buffet, and she saw Don and Tina, but no sign of anyone else; Lydia did not seem to be there.

Marigold, with a plate of food, found a quiet spot halfway up the enormous staircase. She was not alone, however. Jenny Warren was standing by the banisters, looking down into the hall full of people. She looked wretched.

"Jenny! You're here! Barrie said you weren't well."

"I'm fine."

But she looked terrible. Marigold put her arm around her and steered her along the upstairs corridor until she found a quiet space, a small dressing room lit by scented candles. Moroccan cushions covered the floor, and there were floating draperies. A cool breeze blew in from the sea.

They sat down and Marigold offered Jenny her plate. "Why don't you have something to eat and tell me what's wrong."

Jenny shook her head, her fair hair tumbling about her face. A few minutes later, she was crying quietly. "We had a row," she said, tears trickling down her cheeks. "At least, Barrie was angry with me, but I can't remember how it started. I must have said something, or done something... Anyway, he was fed up with me and when I was round his flat this morning doing the cleaning—"

"You were what?"

"I—I clean his flat. He can't look after himself, he's got so many other things to think about. And he's always so grateful. I actually quite like cleaning."

Marigold had a flashback to Barrie's flat—the spotless cleanliness, the vases of flowers. Jenny drudging in her spare time.

"I know what you're thinking, I know he's not the faithful type. He can't help being charming, just like Lord Harcourt. That's probably why he can do the part so brilliantly."

"Yes, but that's onstage. Jenny, why do you put up with him?"

"I love him." She put her head in her hands and wept. "I'd do anything for him. Last season he had other—well, there were other people but, in the end, they all went away and he came back to me. And he's always so sorry about how weak he is. I know he cares, deep down. I know he values his independence. He's told me how terrified he is of commitment, of being trapped into marriage..."

"Oh, right," said Marigold. She wondered what version of himself he was at this moment presenting to Betsy. She felt a surge of anger. She was going to have to do something.

"Jenny, wait here. I'll get Barrie. He's here somewhere. Eat some food and stop crying. I promise he'll come and find you."

"Oh, Marigold, thank you. I'd be so grateful."

Marigold retraced her steps to the ballroom. The band was playing a slow number now, and the frenzied bopping of earlier on had given way to a sensuous languor as couples, bodies locked together, swayed to the music. Around the edge of the room, other couples were writhing in abandoned embraces, oblivious to everything. Marigold threaded her way through, stepping over bodies, looking for Betsy and Barrie. She dreaded having to physically force them apart.

Eventually she found them up near the band, still upright, dancing together. Betsy's head was buried in Barrie's shoulder, and his hand was stroking down her back, softly, rhythmically. Her eyes were closed. They were as close as two bodies can be.

Marigold hovered near them, wondering what her next move should be, awkwardness replacing her earlier anger. Maybe she should wait until the music ended. She moved away, and was grabbed by a strong pair of arms that crushed her to a navy blue jacket—could it be Tor? She raised her eyes to a total stranger with a bald head and a thin face, and pulled away angrily.

"Oh, sorry!" he said sarcastically. "Who let you out of playschool?" And he wandered away, dragging on his cigarette, leaving Marigold pink with embarrassment.

Betsy and Barrie were kissing now, erotically and lingeringly, pressed against each other, barely moving to the music. Betsy's dress was slipping from her shoulder, and Barrie's hand was on her breast. It seemed as if the music was never going to end.

Marigold took a deep breath and put her hand on Barrie's shoulder, squeezing it as hard as she could. He jumped back, and she grabbed hold of Betsy, wishing she had some cold water to throw over her.

"Barrie has to be somewhere else," she said, trying to sound authoritative.

"No, he doesn't," said Betsy. "He's with me tonight."

Barrie was smiling in an infuriating way, standing back, with his arms folded. The music finally came to an end and Marigold raised her voice.

"Jenny's here."

Barrie shrugged. "So?"

"She's upset."

"I told you, she's not well. She should have had an early night."

"She wants to talk to you, Barrie."

Barrie made a little face to Betsy, as if apologizing for this interruption. When he turned back to Marigold, his face had the sulky small boy look that Marigold had seen before. "Then let her come and find me."

Marigold got in between him and Betsy. "Can I just have one word with you in private?" she asked her friend.

"Don't run away," said Betsy, kissing Barrie on the cheek. "Remember, we have a date."

Marigold hustled her to a brightly lit area, with no idea what to do next. "Betsy, you have to listen to me."

"Tomorrow."

"Jenny's a sweet person and he is wrecking her head—"

"I'm not listening…" sang Betsy, who had obviously had a few drinks. "I've only got one night to make a move, and I am not giving up a very, very special moment because my friend is jealous."

"I am *so* not jealous!"

"Barrie's told me about Jenny. She's stalking him, she is infatuated with him, she's a sad case—but she is not his responsibility."

"Betsy, please, don't get involved with Barrie."

"Oh, easy for you to say that—you've got your job. He's got influence. He's got friends making films for Channel 4. He can get me a part in the next series of *Street Life*. He's promised to put my name on the casting director's desk. I'll be on telly!"

"You haven't fallen for that!"

"Why would he lie to me?"

"Er, to get you into bed?"

"He doesn't have to promise me anything to make me go to bed with him. I'm the adventurous, gypsy type he has dreamed of meeting all his life. We are meant to be together."

Betsy turned and left. Marigold felt a chill of despair seize her. This was an impossible task.

She went back to Jenny, still crouching hopefully on the Moroccan cushions.

"Did you see him?" she asked. "Is he coming?"

"Well, not exactly. We have to go and find him."

Jenny got up. "Thank you, Marigold. I'm so glad you're here. You won't leave me on my own, will you?"

"No," said Marigold glumly. "Are you sure you want to do this? He's with my friend. They're dancing."

"I don't care who he's with. I want to see him."

"You could get hurt."

Jenny's face was uncharacteristically hard as she said, "Not more than I've been hurt already."

But Barrie and Betsy weren't in the ballroom. They searched all the rooms on the ground floor, with no luck.

"Maybe they've left," said Marigold. That would leave her and Jenny stranded.

"Oh, I feel so tired," Jenny said, looking weepy again. "I just have to sit down for a moment."

"I'll go upstairs and out on the balcony, then I can see if Barrie's car is still in the drive," said Marigold, wondering if this evening was ever going to end.

There were more people arriving, and more food being delivered to the tables, and the music was starting up again, but Marigold made her way upstairs and out onto the balcony, where the air was fresh and sweet. Apart, that is, from the smell of cigarette smoke. A figure was there, leaning over the balustrade.

It was Barrie.

There was no sign of Betsy. As if guessing her thoughts, he said, in his husky voice, "She's gone to the ladies' room."

Marigold took a step toward him. "Listen to me. Please don't leave here with Betsy. She's my best friend. She doesn't need this."

"She's an adult. I'm not Derren Brown. I can't make her do anything she doesn't want to."

There was a quiet movement in the shadows, but Marigold, her face framed in the full moonlight, was too intent to pay attention to anything but Barrie's mocking mouth.

"Barrie, don't, I beg you. Don't be so cruel. Do you enjoy breaking hearts like this? I can't bear it, watching you seducing my best friend...and I stupidly introduced her to you! Now you're kissing her and pretty well having sex with her on the dance floor. After what you said to me when we were in your flat—"

"I don't remember what we said, only that your mouth was very soft—"

A tall figure moved out of the shadows. Marigold spun round to see Tor, his eyes blazing.

"Listen to her, Barrie," he said, and the suppressed fury in his voice made her shudder. "She's begging you for a second chance. Why don't you take pity on her?"

Marigold staggered back against the balustrade. "Tor...I didn't know you were here."

His lip curled disdainfully. "That much is obvious."

Before she could stop him, he was moving toward Barrie. His anger was so glacial, so terrifying, that Barrie's poise was shaken. His mouth opened, but no words came out. He took a step back, as if afraid that Tor was going to hit him.

Tor ignored Marigold and spoke to Barrie again. "Don't worry, she isn't worth fighting over. Take her and welcome."

And he was gone.

CHAPTER ELEVEN

As if in a dream, Marigold followed Tor's progress from the balcony. She saw him, pale with fury, emerging from the house, scattering the other guests before him. He got into a black car and drove recklessly away, speeding down the drive, scattering gravel in all directions.

After he left, there was a brief moment of deathly silence.

Then all her strength left her and she crumpled to the ground, wishing she could go to sleep and never wake up.

Betsy came to her rescue, and Barrie too, after he had recovered his equilibrium, but their clumsy attempts at comforting her only made the pain more savage. How would she ever get Tor to hear the truth? His grim face and tightly clenched jaw brooked no argument; whatever she told him, he would think she was lying.

Betsy had been sharply brought back to reality by Marigold's distress, and realizing the claims of her old friendship weighed more than the pleasures of a night with Barrie, she called a taxi and they both went home, leaving Barrie to find Jenny and apologize to her, as he promised he would.

All the way home in the taxi, as Betsy cuddled her and gave her paper hankies, Marigold sobbed her heart out. It was too cruel, after that tantalizingly brief phone call when Tor had told her he loved her, that it was now all over; she would never lie next to him again, never see that face made naked and vulnerable, never feel that strong mouth pressed passionately against hers. And how would they be able to work together for the rest of the summer? How could they even bear to be in the same room together?

No wonder Tor had been reluctant to get involved with someone working in the same company. When it went wrong, it was a double disaster. But because he was right about that, and so many other things, what chance did she have of persuading him he had been wrong in his judgement of her, listening in the shadows to a fragmented conversation he had completely misunderstood?

They finally arrived back at Marigold's digs. Betsy made coffee and they sat on Marigold's bed, wrapped up in duvets.

"Do you want to tell me what happened, or shall I just keep handing over the tissues?" asked Betsy.

"I don't understand. Is it possible that you can switch off loving someone in an instant? He seemed as if he hated me back there. As if he wished he'd never set eyes on me."

"Too deep for me, kid," said Betsy. "But if he is as fair as you've told me he is, surely he would give you at least a hearing?"

"We've got to work together on Monday! It's going to be agony. Should I call in sick?"

"Only you know the answer to that one. Is this really the Marigold Aubrey who was scared of nothing? The one who did the bungee jump in Scotland and the parachute thing for charity? Come on, girl. You could go and see him at his hotel tomorrow. I'll be there to hold your coat."

"Never. I'd rather die."

"Oh, now it's life or death. You really do love Tor, don't you?"

Marigold hadn't thought she had any tears left, but "love" and "Tor" in the same breath made her burst out again.

Betsy said impulsively, "How about I go and see him, and tell him what was really going on?"

"I wouldn't wish that on anyone. He'll just see you as another lying actress."

"Oh, thanks a bunch," said Betsy. "Now, can I remind you what you said in my flat the night you got the job? It was going to be career first, remember? No romance? How about going back to Plan A? To hell with men! To hell with Tor Douglas!"

*

Sunday was a brilliant sunny morning, and in spite of their late night, Marigold and Betsy woke early. After breakfast, they decided to wander around town for a bit and then, if it stayed fine, go to the beach until it was time for Betsy's train back to London.

But walking around Branchester, at every turn Marigold came face to face with another reminder of Tor—the shop in the Alleys where he had freed the linnet, the Italian coffee shop where she had spilled coffee all over her best clothes and refused Tor's date. How had he really felt, underneath his confident façade? Had she hurt him that day? Had he already been attracted to her then?

They came out of the Alleys and crossed the road where the Sovereign Hotel's flag fluttered in the warm breeze. Tor's room was there, at the front. He might at this moment be staring out of the window, watching her.

"Changed your mind about popping in and having it out with him right now?" asked Betsy with a grin.

"No thanks, let's move swiftly on."

But images of Tor's room rose before her: the disorder, the piles of scripts and papers, the black sheets, and bright red pajamas—and rehearsing the kiss. His unpredictability—so terrifying, so fascinating—and his kindness and patience that night...

"Marigold—you are not actually moving. Sure you don't want to wander in and have lunch and like, accidentally bump into him?"

"NO! I *am* moving. To the beach."

"Pity. I think I would enjoy meeting the ogre today."

They bought a picnic and wandered toward the shore. It was crowded and too noisy, so they walked further, until there was only sea and space and quietness.

"And what about this spot? Bring back any memories?" asked Betsy affectionately.

"Of course. This is where he taught me how to skim pebbles."

"Ah, bless! He's managed to spoil each and every bit of Branchester for you in three short weeks."

"Look, if you don't shut it I will push you in the sea before you've got your costume on."

"Ooh, Tor Douglas tactics! Okay, I am getting changed! Race you!"

In spite of the sun, the sea was bitingly cold and there were strong waves that tossed the girls about like corks. Marigold loved the crash of the breakers on the shifting stones; it suited her grey and stormy emotions.

Betsy was, after all, a good friend. She said a heartfelt "sorry" for her part in the previous night's misadventures, and made a genuine offer to stay with Marigold for a few extra days, even though it meant missing work and wasting her return ticket.

So it was with reconciliation and mutual affection that the two girls said goodbye at the station, leaving Marigold to shoulder a burden of loneliness and a growing sense of dread about the coming week.

After Betsy had gone, Marigold spent the rest of the evening in her room, making up imaginary witty, adult, scintillating dialogue that she would never actually dare to speak when she next met the man who had said he loved her.

*

Monday morning arrived, and with it the dreadful and unavoidable reality of the day's rehearsal. Marigold was too wrought up to go and do her warm-ups; she put off going to the theatre until the last possible moment, so that by the time she entered, she hoped everyone else would be there and she could slip into the room unnoticed.

Tor must have had plenty of practice at this, she thought grimly, for he was perfectly self-possessed, perfectly polite, and cool to everyone. But Marigold noticed that he never once looked her directly in the eye. Nor did he call her by her own name, but only by the name of her character—and then, only when it was essential. She felt at times as if she was a ghost. But at least it was possible for them to work together in this disconnected, limbo state, and for that she was grateful.

There was only one moment when everything slid out of control.

They were doing detailed character work, and Tor had asked each of them to find the "key." For some characters, it was found in a long speech, for others, maybe only a few words or a gesture. The key encapsulated the spirit of the character, and finding it was of enormous help to an actor. Marigold had found her key speech, and, inevitably, her turn came and she was asked for it. She found she could not meet his eyes, but said the lines looking down at the floor:

"Love may be a poison—but I make my lovers long for it, feeding it in such sweet small doses that they return again and again for more—so how can I be to blame for their slow deaths? I have only given them what they want."

She stopped. There was dead silence. She was forced to look at Tor.

He was staring directly at her now, with a burning contempt in his eyes.

She flung up her chin.

"Of course, that is not how I think life or love should be, as myself," she found herself saying. "In fact, one friend told me my sense of honor was old-fashioned, like something out of *Brief Encounter*."

Tor, without a smile or a change in his expression, said ironically, "A film, I believe, that glorifies adultery? Your friend, I hope, will think again."

Someone in the cast let out their breath in a long, low whistle. Tor swept the moment along with such momentum that no one else had time to react.

Lunchtime came, and Marigold left the room with the other actors, desperate to get away from Tor.

Barrie tried to take her arm, but she pulled away.

"Haven't you done enough damage?"

"I want to help, that's all. Shall I go and talk to him, tell him the truth, even though I don't come out of it smelling of roses?"

"You think he'd believe you, if he didn't believe me?" said Marigold scornfully.

"I feel responsible."

"You *are* responsible. Pity you didn't realize that a long time ago."

Jenny was ahead of them, and Barrie ran off to her and gave her a passionate hug, which she returned. They walked on together, Jenny gazing up adoringly at Barrie, love shining from her eyes. *She's forgiven him*, thought Marigold. *He's lost nothing, but I've lost everything.*

She couldn't face lunch with the others, so she wandered along the beach, wishing she had the courage to hand in her resignation. That was the only future for her now—to cut her losses, personal and professional, go back to London, and try again.

That afternoon, Tor's calmness and coolness was replaced by tempests of anger; nearly every member of the cast came in for a tirade, for the smallest of faults. Lydia and Marigold were so on edge that when it came to the fight, they made a mess of it. They tried it again, and it was a disaster—with Tor standing over them they lost their nerve, missing blows, corpsing, and finally grinding to a halt with him only inches away.

"Bad, bad, bad. Rubbish, the pair of you. Sit down."

They sat, like disgraced schoolgirls, while he lashed them with his tongue.

"We spend the whole morning working on character, but as soon as you two start fighting, you abandon your roles and simply walk through it. That's second rate work—you're wasting my time and everyone else's."

Marigold felt a flash of anger and she didn't stop to think before she answered, "Maybe if our director didn't miss so many crucial rehearsals our concentration would be improved."

There was an audible gasp from Helen and Jenny, and Lydia looked at Marigold with something very like respect.

Not so Tor. With a face like thunder, he flung one of the small tables with all the force he possessed the length of the room. It hit the wall and splintered.

"Tea break," said Tor through clenched teeth, but Marigold stayed where she was. Everyone else scattered.

Even now, with his face white and tense with anger, she longed to put her arms around him. She had to struggle to hold still.

Tor took a few deep breaths, and, when he was calmer, he turned toward her. "I accept the truth of your comment," he said with frigid politeness, "and I can guarantee it will not happen again."

He turned and went to the door, where he delivered his exit line. "We'll run the fight again after the break. I'd advise you to remove that necklace. It could get broken."

Marigold's hand went to her neck. Since he had given her the marigold necklace, she had worn it constantly. But it was a reminder of a moment he now obviously wanted to forget.

The rest of the rehearsal was an anti-climax, apart from one disturbing interlude.

Marigold was the last to leave. She was going downstairs, hoping for a few hours' rest before her last performance as Polly, but Lydia intercepted her.

"I think we should have a little talk, don't you?"

"I have nothing to say to you, Lydia."

"But I have a few juicy morsels to share with you."

"Oh, really?"

"Yes, really. London. Tor and me. The future. Ah, I have your attention now, I think?"

Marigold dragged herself to the green room. Lydia was in no hurry—she spent a long time finding her cigarettes, lighting up, lying down on the couch, and patting a space where she intended Marigold to sit, but Marigold shook her head and remained standing.

"Oh, she's very much on her high horse today," trilled Lydia. "A broken heart adds hugely to our dramatic power, doesn't it?"

"Just say what you want to say, and get it over with, please."

"I think it's time we laid our cards on the table, don't you?"

"I don't have any cards and I don't play games."

Lydia suddenly snapped herself upright. "Nor do I. I told you not to waste his time," she hissed. "And now I'm going to tell you where I spent Friday night."

"If you must," said Marigold, feeling a sick dread in her belly. Lydia was too clever to lie.

"At Tor's flat. We had a most interesting time. Covered a lot of ground we had not previously explored."

"And did you know he phoned me after midnight on Friday night?"

Lydia waved her hand dismissively. "I don't keep tabs on the man—I'm not his nanny. A man as virile as Tor needs the occasional distraction."

"Is that it? Because I'm finding the atmosphere in here too poisonous to breathe."

"So, we have an understanding? Tor's had enough of your schoolgirl crush. He deserves better. So, from now on, it's hands off. Do I make myself clear?"

"If you want a fight, a real fight—fine. I'm not scared of threats from you. I can stand my ground."

Lydia sprang to her feet with a feline power and her beautiful, cruel face became a savage mask. "To the death it is, then. May the best *actress* win."

*

It was time for the last performance of *The Reluctant Rake*.

What a long way we've come, thought Marigold as she put on her makeup and Polly's uniform for the very last time. *Maybe tonight will be my last here, anyway. Lydia's got her sights trained on me, Tor is out of his mind with rage and ready to sack me, and I don't think I can take any more of this theatre, and this bunch of people.*

She went into the wings with a fatalistic feeling that it really did not matter what she did tonight. So much for her drama school training, her enthusiasm, and her ideals! Real life was a lot more complex.

The curtain went up. At first, it seemed as if everything was normal. Lydia had prepared no booby traps for the first scene and as the play went on, the audience laughed and clapped, and in the wings, everyone was quiet and focused.

After the interval, Marigold relaxed a little. It was nearly over, and Tor was not out there watching, because if he had been, Jenny would have come to the dressing room and told them.

They got to Polly's final scene—the letter scene. Marigold was onstage, searching feverishly through the bureau to find the love letter from Lord Harcourt. It was a prop that Jenny had made, with old-fashioned calligraphy and a red blob of sealing wax.

But tonight it looked different. As she unfolded it, she saw that someone had replaced it with another letter altogether. It was written in unfamiliar modern handwriting, in red ink. The scrawled message said, *Black satin sheets are so sexy, aren't they?*

It wrecked Marigold's concentration, just as Lydia had planned—her thoughts whirled back to Tor's room, his smile, the kiss—but with a supreme effort she forced it all to the back of her mind as she tore the letter to shreds, as rehearsed. She was Polly, she was finding Lord Harcourt unfaithful, she was living in 1750, she was a maid...

Lydia entered as Lady Sophie, as innocent and lovely as a young maid in sprigged muslin could be. Her eyes, when they fell on Polly, may have been triumphant slits, but to the audience she presented a face of wide-eyed innocence.

Lydia then brought her second weapon into play—she abandoned all the planned moves and put herself upstage, so Polly would have to turn her back on the audience for most of the scene.

Well, ha ha, Lydia, thought Marigold. *This is something I have been taught to deal with. When we heard at drama school about actors doing this in performance, we all thought how wicked, and how unlikely it would be to meet this in real life—and here is Lydia thinking she's going to make me forget everything, my lines, my moves, my character.*

As Polly, Marigold moved downstage and delivered all her lines straight to the audience. It worked perfectly well, as long as she found props to move and curtains to twitch downstage. Lydia soon realized she was wasting her time and began to go back to the rehearsed moves.

Marigold knew she was not yet home safe, because Lydia seemed to be wanting to get very close to Polly. For Lady Sophie's triumphant speech, where she sends Polly off with a flea in her ear, Lydia came so close to Marigold she could reach out and touch her. She delivered her lines in a waspish, half-amused stage whisper that made Polly's tears seem ridiculous.

"That you have the impertinence to call it love, this mooning and sickness toward a man far above your station—"

Unseen by the audience, Lydia dug Marigold in the back as she spoke, with those long nails that had already drawn blood. Marigold felt the pain, but more painful was the venom in Lady Sophie's voice: "—but that you, a common serving maid, set yourself beside the proper object of his adoration, myself—" The talons pressed the point home; Tor did not want a schoolgirl crush, he wanted Lydia, at the top of her game as an actor, and an invincible force as a lover. "—that, I will not endure!"

As she ended her speech, Lydia, with a vicious tug, pulled at Marigold's necklace, broke the chain, and with a contemptuous gesture, flung it on the floor.

Marigold spun round, and before she could stop herself, raised her hand and gave Lydia a stinging slap on her cheek. The audience gasped. The slap resounded all over the auditorium.

Lydia's mouth dropped open.

After the slap, Marigold bent and picked up the necklace, and unrehearsed words came tumbling out: "He loves me! Not you! Do not delude yourself! And I return his love with all my heart!"

She did not wait for Lydia's final line "You are dismissed" but marched to the exit with her head high. As she reached the door, she turned and looked her last on Lady Sophie, giving her a blazing look of white-hot anger, before sweeping from the stage.

She hardly heard the vigorous round of applause that greeted her exit.

"Well, well!" Helen had been waiting to enter and had seen it all. "You really showed Her Majesty, didn't you?"

"Oh my God, what have I done?" said Marigold, feeling only elation and joy that she had spoken her truth, even if Tor hadn't heard it.

"You've done something no one else has ever dared do, though plenty would have liked to. She's never had her face slapped—and what a slap! Oh, sorry, that's my cue—buy you a drink after!" And Helen sailed on.

Barrie was there too, in fits of laughter.

"Oh, Barrie—I forgot the audience! Do you think they had a clue what was happening?"

"They adored it! Best theatre I've seen in my life!"

Barrie also disappeared onstage.

Marigold's elation ebbed away. It must have been obvious to the audience what was going on. She and Lydia had played out a private vendetta and abandoned all the stage directions Tor had given them. He would be furious if he knew.

Jenny Warren came running over. "Tor's out front—I didn't have time to tell you before."

"Oh God!" said Marigold. "That's it, then. I'm out of a job."

She took her place in the final curtain call, which was extremely enthusiastic. Clearly the audience had enjoyed the show, even the unrehearsed scenes. As they filed offstage, they all saw Tor, standing grimly in the wings.

His arm shot out and caught Lydia; his other arm pinned Marigold. "I'll see you first in my office, Lydia," he said. "Marigold—fifteen minutes."

He and Lydia disappeared down the corridor and Marigold went to her dressing room and, for the last time, changed out of her maid's costume.

Helen made her some tea, looking happier than Marigold had ever seen her. "She's been asking for that for years and years. She's a predator, a man-thief. Took my boyfriend just after we'd got engaged, snatched him away, and he wasn't the only one. I've seen it happen time after time. No one's ever been able to stand up to her—except Tor, of course. And now you."

But was Tor really standing up to her? Lydia was with him now, no doubt getting in her version of the story.

Fifteen minutes later, Marigold was knocking on the door of his office. She hadn't been in this room since her audition.

Tor was leaning back in the swivel chair as he had done the first time she had met him. His arms were folded, and his head was slightly thrown back as he looked her up and down. She could not read the expression on his face.

"Maybe you're not too small for the part, after all," he said.

"What part?"

He said gently, "The part of Mrs. Douglas."

Her heart skipped a beat. "Who's she?"

"My wife. I'm asking you to marry me." He got up from the chair. He lifted Marigold onto the table and looked up into her face. "Will you marry me?"

"I—Tor—I—this is the last thing I was expecting."

"Good," he said. "I'd hate to become predictable."

She knelt down so their faces were level, and his hands came up to stroke her cheeks. Their lips pressed together in a kiss as soft and sweet as the breath of a sleeping baby.

He took his mouth away to whisper, "I love you. Love, love you."

She wanted to kiss him back, wanted to say yes, wanted him there and then, but though she loved him with all of her heart and soul and body, she could not give herself away in a second to a man who had hurt her so much, so confused her, mystified her, and played with her as he had.

She lifted up his head, tilting his chin so their eyes met. She felt his surrender to her. "Tor, you have to talk to me. You have to tell me what you've been doing."

"I know, I know. Let's sit down."

He sat in the swivel chair, inviting her to join him, but she shook her head and perched on the edge of the table, where she could look into his eyes as an equal.

"First of all, let me say sorry in any way you want, for Saturday. That dreadful party. I only went there to find you. I'd driven back from London to give you something, and I was so wrought up, so over-excited, that I grossly misunderstood the situation. I judged you appallingly, with no evidence, and I behaved in a way that I can only describe as shameful."

"How did you find out the truth? Barrie?"

"Barrie, my arse! It was Jenny. She had no idea you and I were—well, anyway, it wasn't until just before the show went up tonight that she and I had a talk. I always listen to Jenny. From now on, I'll always listen to you. If you're still willing to talk to me."

"You said you had something to give me?"

He opened the desk drawer and took out a box. It was from the same jewellers in Branchester, and it was the same size as the box with the necklace. Slowly, looking at her, he opened it. There was a ring inside. He put it on the table next to her. But she did not pick it up. Before she could let herself do that, she had to know the answer to the question that was tearing her heart in two.

"Why did you disappear without a word on my birthday? Lydia says she was in London with you. At your flat. Is that true?"

He held her look.

"Yes, she was."

"She hinted that she stayed the night with you. Suggested that you'd slept with her. Did you? "

"No. Never in the world would I do that." Tor's voice rose passionately. Marigold wanted so much to believe him, to trust him—or their love would be based on falsehood. As she held his look, nearly falling into his arms, but resisting, something deep in her knew he would always tell her the truth, however difficult it was. She suddenly remembered Don saying, "Tor is straight and he never lies."

" Lydia was there," he said. "But did she tell you we weren't alone? Her new agent was with her, negotiating, wheeling and dealing. She came for business, not pleasure. And she left with him."

"Her agent?"

"Yes, Saul Eckstein, a big shot, apparently, from Hollywood. You may have seen him out front tonight—tall dude, silver hair and a smug expression."

"I saw him get off the train with Lydia. So he was in your flat too?"

"He was the whole reason she was there. She has at last got the stardom she's been wanting all her life, signed for a lead role in the Coen brothers' next movie. I saw the gold-plated contract. And that means far more to Lydia than a dead-end dalliance with me."

"Okay...but why so late at night?"

"Because he'd just arrived from L.A, and in his mind it was the afternoon. I'd only just got in the door when he rang. And even though I was desperate to get back to you, I had to get it sorted out."

He stood up, and bowed his head.

"I won't blame you if you walk away now."

Marigold slid from the table, lifted her face to him, and kissed him—not gently, but hard, as suspicions, judgements, and all the mysteries of the past began to roll away.

"I'm still here," she said. "But there's a lot you haven't explained. I have to know what I am taking on—who I'm taking on. Are there more secrets? What about your other wives? "

Tor went and stood by the window, looking out at the fading day.

"I was married twice. Once, hundreds of years ago to Janette Taylor—we were both kids, it lasted a year, we divorced. Then I got together with Sandra Cadell—well, actually, she was my divorce lawyer. She was sane, realistic, not an actor. In fact, she very wisely refused to marry me. I thought I'd found my soul mate. She found out she'd shackled herself to an alcoholic."

"An alcoholic?"

He sighed, turning to look at her, as sadly as if he'd already lost her.

"Yes, I was. Not now, not any more. After Sandra left me, and I didn't blame her, I drank my way through a series of relationships—and how I stayed in work, I'll never know. I never missed a day of rehearsal. I was never late for curtain up, never fell down in the street, but I was actually quite mad, for years. Five years ago, after nearly killing myself in an accident, I stopped drinking. Now I'm sober and, darling, I promise you, I always will be. Unfortunately, before that happened, I had met Blanche. I loved her because she was so tolerant, so understanding. She never accused me of being drunk and incapable, she was sweet and loving, but..."

"But?" Marigold went over to him and stood beside him. She felt that she held him in the palm of her hand. He knew what he risked losing by telling her all this. No one could say Tor Douglas was a coward.

"But she was a total addict. Drink, big time. Brandy for breakfast. Bottles under the bed. Concealment. Appalling sessions in public when I had to carry her home and pay for damage and—it was hell. And once I'd stopped drinking, she stopped being an angel."

He fell silent. Marigold stroked his hair back from his face, kissing his forehead. The lines of pain eased away.

"We were married—plenty of champagne, of course, and Blanche's father was delighted that his wild child was safe in my capable hands. He was a formidable old businessman, and I knew nothing about business, nor was I interested in money, but when my parents died I'd inherited a bit, and he persuaded me to invest it in something or other, which I did, and we signed a contract. I didn't even run it by a solicitor, but it bound me to Blanche and her family. If I'd read the small print I would have run a mile. "

He was looking at her now, with troubled eyes.

"Telling you all this is the hardest thing I've ever done. But how can you say 'yes' to an emotional cripple who keeps his ugly secrets hidden? Just remember, please, my darling, that I wasn't much older than you when all this was going on. Awful things started happening. Blanche was an actor, but never in work, so she stayed home drinking while I tried to earn a crust. I came home one evening and our flat had been trashed. It was Blanche—she'd had a psychotic episode. She was totally out of reach. I was scared, she was terrified, I didn't know what to do, I stayed up all night trying to calm her down. About five in the morning, she was suicidal, and I had to hold her while I phoned her parents. Her father wasn't surprised, because she'd done this before, only no one thought to tell me. He told me she was my responsibility and put the phone down. I had to call the ambulance, and I had to take the steps to get her sectioned, because she wouldn't go in as a voluntary patient. That was the most hellish night of my life. I felt as if I was in a black pit of hell. Utterly alone, with darkness and wild things attacking me on all sides..."

"This isn't making me love you less," said Marigold, with tears in her eyes. No wonder she had seen such pain in his face on the night they had made love. No wonder he was sometimes so angry.

"Well, after that, it was a sad catalogue of Blanche drying out, coming out of hospital, falling off the wagon, harming herself, going inside again, and all the time I was the only person who kept in contact with her. I was the one they called when she'd had another crisis, and when someone like her has a crisis, you drop everything. That's why I had to go to London on Friday night."

"Because of Blanche?"

"Yes, but this time it was finally something good. She's out of hospital. She's sober. She's met a sweet, wonderful man—she wanted a divorce so she could marry him. All I had to do was be there and sign the papers. Which was a huge relief."

Tor squeezed Marigold so passionately that the air rushed out of her lungs in a loud "ah!" of surprise.

He looked remorseful. "Oh, God, darling! I haven't hurt you, have I? Tell me if I'm being a brute—"

"You're never a brute."

"So kind. That Friday, at seven, was the only time we could all get together—her father was there, my solicitor, her fiancé, Blanche, my accountant—so we could undo the contract, set the decree in motion, and finally draw a line under the whole business. I knew that if I didn't, I would never be able to marry you, never be able to tell you how I felt about you, because it wouldn't be fair. I wouldn't be free. And I was longing to be free. The meeting took three hours, and as soon as it was over, I remembered I'd promised to take you away. I was going to phone you as soon as I got back to the flat, but that's when Eckstein rang and he and Lydia came round. I didn't have a minute to myself. I didn't forget you, I—"

She interrupted him with a kiss, then more kisses; questions seemed to be answering themselves, and knots were unraveling until Marigold felt as if she was in a real-life fairytale pantomime, where the wicked get punished and Cinderella gets her prince. But Tor was no prince. She was beginning to understand her man, troubled though he was.

"If I hadn't been in such a state of madness when I arrived at that bloody party I might have engaged my brain before jumping to conclusions. I know now that you turned Barrie down, not the other way round. I know you're too intelligent to trust him—why couldn't I have trusted you?"

"Tor, you realize that all this misery could have been avoided if you'd had a mobile phone?" said Marigold.

He ran his hands through his hair, in that gesture she loved. "Ah! She's going to reform me! The old dinosaur is being dragged kicking and screaming into the right century…"

"You could have texted and explained why you had to go to London on my birthday. And I could have talked to you. I'd have known what was going on."

"But I'd lose all my mystery," he said, kissing her palm. "The fact is, I've been on my own for so long, there wasn't anyone I needed to be in touch with. There was no one in the world I cared about." He sighed, tracing the outline of her brow with one finger. "I'll get one tomorrow. But don't ask me to do fancy stuff with the hellish thing. Carol will be delighted. And Jenny. They've been nagging me for years."

Marigold took up the ring and held it in her palm.

"I need to say sorry to you, too. I did a really bad thing tonight, in that last scene. I'm sorry I slapped Lydia in front of the audience."

"Well, I'm delighted you did! It was a wonderful moment! Echoed round the auditorium like a pistol shot!"

Tor began to laugh. *Does he know if he's won me?* She wondered.

"I found a message from her, in red ink, on Lord Harcourt's letter. How did she know about your sexy black sheets?"

"Oh, because she gave me the horrible things. A sly 'thank you, and let's see what this leads to' kind of present for renewing her contract here. They came by special delivery, with a highly suggestive note attached."

"I thought you must be a very decadent person when I saw them on your bed," said Marigold.

"Decadent! They were so slippery and uncomfortable I threw 'em out after three days and went back to nice white cotton ones."

They both fell silent, remembering the chaos of that room.

"Your room scared me," said Marigold.

"It was symbolic of the mess my life was in at the time. Next time you see it—which I hope will be very soon—you'll feel reassured."

"So Lydia was lying about everything?"

"She's a mistress of half-truths and innuendos. You cannot seriously imagine I would get involved with someone as devious and selfish as her?"

"I wonder what she'll have up her sleeve for me tomorrow," said Marigold, feeling that nothing was too much for her now, even though the name of Lydia Dawlish screamed defiance down at her from the posters on the walls.

"She won't try anything. I've just given her the most almighty telling off for being unprofessional. She knows when she's been beaten."

Marigold took the ring from its box. It was small, white gold, with a single tiny diamond. It looked a perfect fit.

"How did you know my size?" she asked, and a twinkle of mischief came back to his eyes.

"You forget that every single measurement of you, from top to toe, was with Peggy in the wardrobe. All I had to do was tell her I needed Jenny to buy a wedding ring for Amber de Lacey."

"So they knew? Before I did?"

"No, my darling. *I* went and bought that ring. Jenny, Tina, Peggy—none of them knew the real reason. You are the first to know. Do you—do you like it?"

"It's beautiful." Marigold held the ring in the palm of her hand. Had he answered all her questions? Had she made him wait long enough? Oh, the delicious anticipation before she gave her reply! How she wanted to prolong it, just for a moment more.

"You know how I feel, Tor—I don't have to put it into words—"

"But you did! Tonight, onstage! I heard you say you loved me. I saw you outfox the queen of vixens. You were magnificent!"

"I thought you'd called me up here to sack me."

"Sack you? For teaching Lydia a lesson? I could see exactly what she was up to. The better woman won," said Tor, with a fierce pride and joy in his face.

Marigold slipped the ring onto her finger, and held out her hand to him. The ring fit perfectly, and she could not help a childish expression of delight creeping over her face, a look she saw mirrored on his.

"It's yes," she said.

He took a deep breath, and kissed her hand.

"Thank you for—"

"Don't say, 'for trusting me'—you have to get a new line, Tor!" His voice was soft now, intense and low.

"Thank you for listening to me, for understanding me, for loving me, for marrying me. Choose the one that's most appropriate."

"Only all of them," she said, just as softly, which led to another interlude of kisses and crazy, loving endearments.

"How I'd longed for the moment when I would be able to tell you I loved you. Of course Lydia and her agent got in the way, but finally—when was it?"

"Midnight."

"I know it was a mad thing to do. But I had to tell you right then."

"It was wonderful. But it was lots of other things too."

"Hear it again. I love you. I love you, Marigold Aubrey."

As the room began to grow dark, they stood together, looking down on all the lights of Branchester.

"Here's a weird thing," said Tor. "That business deal has paid out a dividend. So—on Saturday, would you like to come and buy a house with me?"

*

They were married as soon as Tor's decree came through, on a mellow, golden autumn day. Everyone was invited, and everyone came. Peggy and Tina adapted one of the wardrobe's costumes for Marigold—a flowing dress in a misty purple-blue shade that brought out the color of her eyes. Tina whipped up a delicious little hat to match. Tor looked dashing in his navy blue suit, and Lydia was stunning in black and white, with a cartwheel of a hat, crying natural and photogenic tears that had the paparazzi snapping madly.

Tor asked Don Burlington to be his best man, and promised to reciprocate when he and Tina got married sometime next year. Betsy was there, of course, with shining eyes, having just landed her first job—in *As You Like It* at the Globe Theatre. Shakespeare, in London! It was what they had both dreamed of—but today, Marigold would not have changed places with her, not for the world. Jenny and Barrie masterminded the catering, with champagne, strawberries out of season, and smoked salmon. Marigold's parents, slightly bemused by the press, photographers, and the crowds of guests, were totally charmed by their new son-in-law.

"I thought you said he was scary and grumpy," Marigold's mother whispered to her at the reception.

"No, Ma, it was you who said that."

"And you're not having a proper honeymoon. Are you sure you're doing the right thing?"

"Ma, I love him."

"He is very personable. What a lovely voice. Why doesn't he go on the stage?"

"No thanks," said Tor, overhearing this. "One actor in the family is quite enough."

*

Who needs a honeymoon? thought Marigold as they went back to the Sovereign after the reception. They'd found their house a month ago—a big Victorian ex-boarding house on the seafront, and though it needed everything doing to make it perfect, they were going to move in as soon as they could. Why worry about furniture? Everything would come, in time.

How did they spend their wedding night? Reading the script for the next production, which had Don's name on it as designer.

"This is a scorcher," said Tor as they sat in the double bed, drinking tea. "You're a fifteen-year-old schoolgirl whose parents are terrorized by the arrival of an evil siren from your father's past. She brings with her a neurotic young lover who of course falls madly and impossibly in love with you. Helen and Barrie will make a good husband and wife—nice part for Helen, she deserves it—and Robin will be the neurotic young lover. Lydia, of course, will play the monster."

"What's it called?"

"*Act of Love*. What do you think?"

"Let's do it," said Marigold.

So they did.

About the Author

Pan Zador has lived and worked in Wales and Ireland. Her life has been spent in theatre as actor, director and playwright. She has kissed many handsome heroes onstage, and married two of them—but not at the same time.

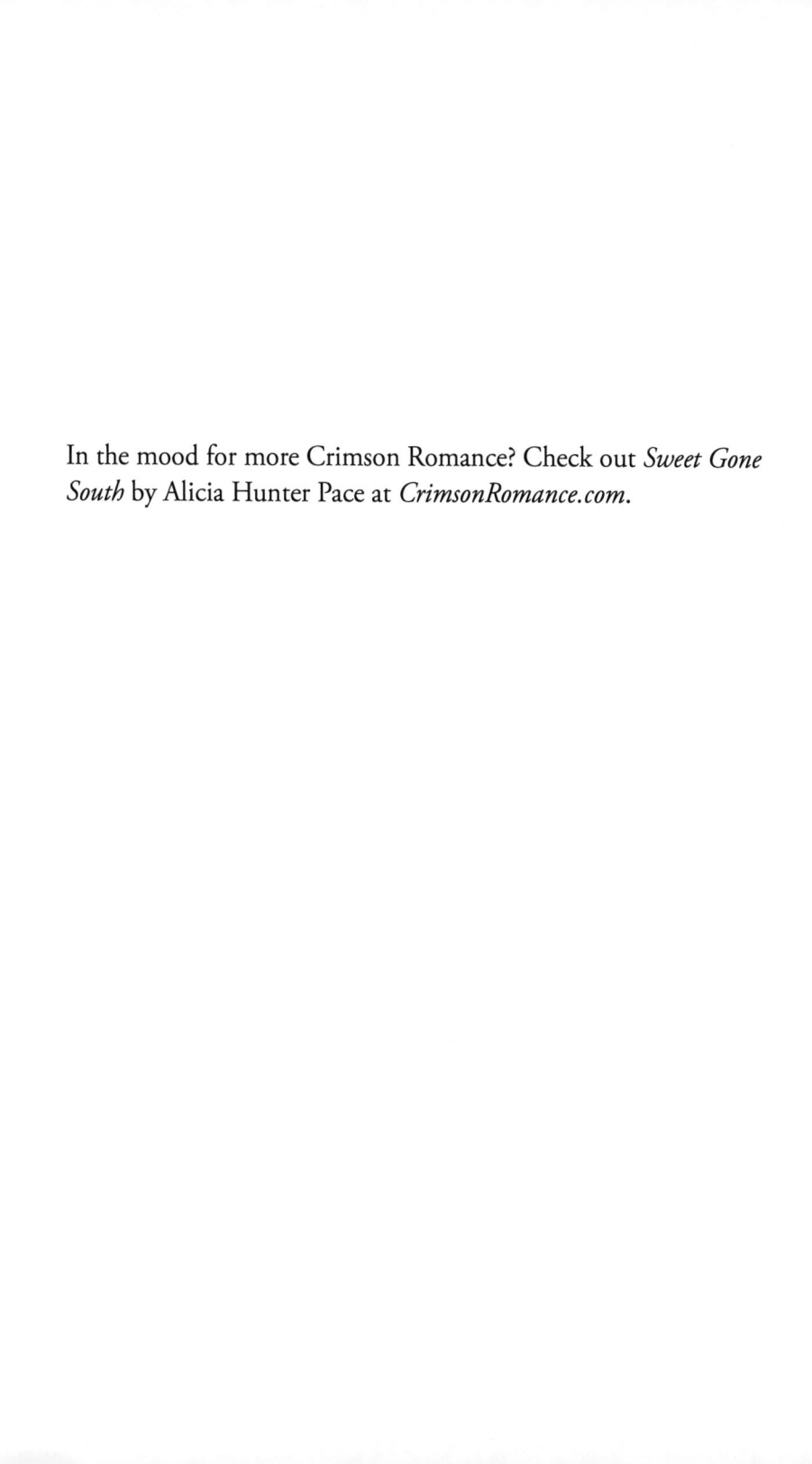

In the mood for more Crimson Romance? Check out *Sweet Gone South* by Alicia Hunter Pace at *CrimsonRomance.com*.